Archibald Granger Bowie

The Romance of the British Post Office

Archibald Granger Bowie

The Romance of the British Post Office

ISBN/EAN: 9783337347130

Printed in Europe, USA, Canada, Australia, Japan

Cover: Foto ©Andreas Hilbeck / pixelio.de

More available books at **www.hansebooks.com**

THE ROMANCE

OF THE

BRITISH POST OFFICE

Its Inception and Wondrous Development

BY

ARCHIBALD GRANGER BOWIE.

"Of all inventions, the alphabet and the printing-press alone excepted, those inventions which abridge distance have done most for the civilisation of our species."—LORD MACAULAY.

LONDON

S. W. PARTRIDGE & CO.

8 & 9 PATERNOSTER ROW.

1897.

AWAITING THE MAIL.

PREFACE.

SINCE the days of Rowland Hill, the great pioneer of postal reform, Post Office business in this country has grown and developed to such a marvellous extent that the system has interwoven itself into the daily life of the people and become one of the most important factors of our social economy. So excellent, too, are the arrangements for the carriage and delivery of the thousands of millions of letters passing through the post every year, that few, probably, pause to think of the great mental and physical strain involved in the maintenance of our huge postal system. Yet the Post Office, with its immense buildings, and large army of busy workers scattered all over the country, as well as its vast and complex organisation, is without doubt one of the wonders of the age. Only those who have had the opportunity of visiting the interior of some of our largest Post Offices can have any idea of what the work, in all its varied branches, really means.

Nevertheless, so closely associated is the business with the interests of almost every individual, that some account of the methods by which it is carried on day by day with such regularity and despatch can hardly fail to appeal attractively to the popular mind. The story, too, of the inception and marvellous development of the system is not devoid of an interest that borders almost on the romantic.

The literature of the Post Office is not extensive, and although some interesting books on the subject have been published—amongst which Lewins's " Her Majesty's Mail," Hyde's " Royal Mail," and Joyce's " History of the Post Office," may be mentioned as standard works—they are not within the reach of all. The present small volume, therefore, is designed to put before the public, in popular form, a succinct narrative of the origin and progress of the British Post Office. And in doing so, the author would take this opportunity of acknowledging his indebtedness to the first two of the above-mentioned works for some few facts, especially with regard to the ancient history of our Post Office.

ARCHIBALD GRANGER BOWIE.

IN THE PNEUMATIC TUBE ROOM.

CONTENTS.

viii   CONTENTS.

CHAPTER VII.

CHAPTER VIII.

CHAPTER IX.

CHAPTER X.

A LONDON POSTMAN—1838.
(*From a Photograph by A. L. Tyler.*)

THE ROMANCE

OF THE

BRITISH POST OFFICE.

———◆———

CHAPTER I.

EARLY HISTORY.

THE establishment of means of inter-communication between individuals and communities living in different parts of a country appears to have been one of the earliest signs of advancing civilisation. At first, messages thus interchanged were purely oral, trusty couriers being employed for the purpose; but it was quickly discovered that communications of this kind were of little value in the case of important despatches, especially for those which required secrecy. As a result, written signs were speedily employed in place of oral communication. Hence we hear of letters and posts from very remote times. It was long, of course, ere the art of writing became known to any considerable extent, and the earliest letters of which we hear were solely on Government business. Indeed, such posts or means of conveyance as existed in those days were simply for the purpose of transmitting State communications, and private individuals were left almost entirely without such facilities, a hardship that was probably not much felt when letter-writing was confined to the very few. Biblical history contains frequent references to both letters and posts, Queen Jezebel being credited with having sent the first circular letter. Naaman, about the year 900 B.C., was the bearer of a letter from his master, the King of Syria, to the King of Israel ; while 200 years later, in the days of Hezekiah, we read that "the *posts* went with the letters from the king and his princes throughout all Israel." Again, in the Book of Esther, we are told that Ahasuerus sent letters into every province concerning his wife, Vashti, informing his subjects that it was his Imperial will that "every man should bear rule in his own house," a precept that is not without its value even in our own day.

Some of the expedients resorted to in the early days of civilisation for the conveyance of secret intelligence were very curious. Perhaps the most remarkable was that related by Herodotus, which was to shave the head of a trusty messenger and impress the message on the scalp. "When the hair had grown sufficiently long for concealment, the messenger proceeded to his destination," and, according to this barbarous arrangement, his head was again shaved and the object of the secret mission revealed. Ovid tells of messages being inscribed on a person's back ; while Josephus states that during some wars messages were conveyed by men disguised as animals, or that they were enclosed in coffins in company with an embalmed body. Appian mentions letters inscribed on leaden bullets and thrown by a sling into a besieged city or camp. Julius Cæsar, and other Roman emperors, employed the modern method of conveying secret intelligence by cypher.

The first idea of anything like a real postal system is due to the Persians, who, in the time of Cyrus, possessed a regular riding post, stations, and men, with horses always in readiness, being appointed at distances that a horse could travel in a day. There were 111 such stages, a day's journey from each other, between Susa and the Ægean Sea, a large and beautiful structure being erected at each stage, with every convenience for the purpose designed. The speed of the couriers was, according to Herodotus, such as "nothing mortal surpassed," and, on the main road from Susa to Sardis, varied, as a matter of fact, from 60 to 120 miles a-day. Herodotus, indeed, appears to have been mightily impressed with this speed, for he adds, "Nothing in the world is borne so swiftly as messages by the Persian couriers." What would he have thought, one wonders, of the modern rate of speed!

The Greeks and the Romans do not appear to have been very forward in the matter of postal communications, and amongst the former, private correspondence is said to have scarcely existed prior to 600 B.C. Sometime subsequently special messengers, or runners, were employed to carry State messages, and one of these, Phidippides, has had his name handed down to posterity, from the circumstance that he ran from Athens to Sparta, a distance of 150

English miles, in two days. In ancient Rome public couriers were instituted by the Emperor Augustus, who organised along the roads, to which great attention was paid, inns or stages, at which relays of horses were appointed. Passing westward it may be mentioned that in the olden empires of Mexico and Peru postal facilities were not overlooked, and the systems which existed in those countries are said to have compared favourably with those of ancient Persia, as well as with Greece and Rome. The Chinese likewise, in their early history, maintained a postal system, principally, however, in the less populous districts and for the conveyance of news over long distances, and which Marco Polo, the celebrated Venetian traveller, who visited China in the fourteenth century, has described as being similar to that in existence in Persia under Cyrus.

This book is, of course, concerned alone with the history of the British Post Office, but it has appeared to the author that the foregoing facts, which have been very briefly narrated, are of considerable interest, as demonstrating that in all countries where any degree of civilisation existed, the necessity of an organised system of postal communication was early recognised as being an essential factor in the progress and prosperity of the nation.

Turning now to our own country, we find that, like all other institutions whose origin dates back into anything like antiquity, the first establishment of a postal service for the conveyance of public letters is involved in much obscurity. It seems tolerably certain that no organised system of posts under Government control was established until the reign of James I., and that prior to that time such posts as existed were purely the result of private enterprise. Originally, indeed, the letters of both private and public personages were sent by special messengers only, and subsequently by common carriers who began to ply regularly with their pack-horses about the time of the Wars of the Roses, a mode of conveyance which must have been exceedingly slow, seeing that these carriers travelled the journey through with the same horses. Nevertheless, this was for a long time the only conveyance available to the public.

It was not until nearly two centuries later that anything like a Government system of posts, that is to say, relays of horses and men under State control, was organised, but, as early as the time of Edward II., we find that private individuals kept horses for hire, so that a messenger might travel post—*i.e.*, by relays, and as "Haste, Post, Haste," is found written on the backs of private letters, at the close of the fifteenth and sixteenth centuries, it is to be assumed that the use of this mode of conveyance was not confined alone to Government correspondence.

In 1481 Edward IV., when at war with Scotland, is said to have established a system of posts between York and Edinburgh, the stations being twenty miles apart, so that the despatches were conveyed 200 miles in three days. But, like many of these early posts, when the occasion which had called the system into existence ceased, the system fell into disuse. In the reign of Queen Elizabeth there would appear to have been posts for the transmission of the public despatches, inasmuch as we hear of one, Thomas Randolph, being Chief Postmaster of England in 1581 ; about this time the first horse posts in Ireland were established for the purpose of bringing intelligence of military events.

As already mentioned, the first Government Letter Post was not established until the reign of James I., who, as is stated by a proclamation of Charles I., set on foot a Post Office for letters to foreign countries, "for the benefit of the English merchants," with the view, it would appear, of settling a dispute that existed between those merchants and the alien merchants residing in London. These latter had, it seems, organised a post of their own from London to the out ports, which the English merchants complained acted unfairly towards them, by keeping back their letters, etc. This post, it will be seen, was for foreign letters only, inland correspondence being still unprovided for, and special messengers continued to be employed for the conveyance of the State letters. It is of interest to observe that, in order to prevent these Crown couriers from loitering on the road, it was customary for each postmaster to endorse on the despatch the hour of the courier's arrival at his post house. A letter of 1623, from the Deputy Mayor of Plymouth to Sir Edward Conway, Secretary of State, is in existence bearing such endorsements. The courier started from Plymouth at 11 A.M., the 17th of June, and arrived in London at 8 P.M. on the 19th.

The obvious advantages of the foreign letter post, no doubt, speedily led to the consideration of the desirability of establishing a similar system for inland correspondence, for, in the next reign, it is recorded that a Post Office for inland letters was instituted. It appears that the unlucky Charles I. was struck with the fact that up to that time there had been no regular system of communication between England

and Scotland, and in the year 1635 he issued orders that his Postmaster of England for foreign parts should arrange a running post or two, to run night and day between Edinburgh and London, to go thither and come back in six days, taking in all letters that might be directed to any post town in or near that road. He also directed that bye-posts should be connected with many places on the main line, so as to provide for the transmission of letters from and to Lincoln, Hull, and other towns. Similarly, there were to be posts to Chester, Holyhead, Exeter, and Plymouth, while it was further given out that as soon as possible like posts should be organised for the Oxford and Bristol road, as well as for the road leading through Colchester to Norwich. The rates to be charged were fixed at 2d. a single letter for any distance under 80 miles ; 4d. up to 140 miles ; and 6d. for any longer distance in England, while to any place in Scotland the charge was 8d.

The system would appear to have been successful, for steps were speedily taken to monopolize the service, and in 1637 it was further ordered by proclamation that no other messengers or foot posts were to carry letters except those employed by the King's Postmaster-General, unless it was to places not touched by the King's posts, and with the exception of common known carriers, or persons carrying a letter for a friend, or messengers sent on purpose. The management of the new establishment was intrusted to the foreign Postmaster, Thomas Witherings by name, a gentleman who did not hold the office very long, for in 1641 he was superseded for alleged abuses in both his offices, which were sequestered and placed in the hands of Philip Burlamachy, who exercised them thenceforth under the superintendence of the principal Secretary of State. It is from this time that the Post Office may be said to have become one of the settled institutions of the country. It is note-worthy, however, that the object of the Crown, in establishing the letter post, appears to have been quite as much for the formation of a profitable monopoly as for the accommodation of the public.

It is not to be imagined that the formation of this monopoly took place without opposition. On the contrary, great dissatisfaction was caused by the circumstance, and the prohibition of the carrying letters by others than persons employed by the King's Postmaster was regarded as an unwarrantable stretch of the royal prerogative, in consequence of which a Committee of the House of Commons was appointed in 1642 to inquire into the matter, while the subject afterwards engaged the attention of Parliament. As was to be expected, the great utility of the institution was too apparent to admit of its being abandoned, and the chief result of the inquiries seems to have been the election in 1644 of Edmund Prideaux, the Chairman of the 1642 Committee, and who subse-quently was Attorney-General to the Commonwealth, to be Chief Postmaster. Prideaux's chief claim to notice in connection with the history of the Post Office appears to be that, by establishing a weekly conveyance of letters into all parts of the Kingdom, he saved the public a charge of £7000 a-year in maintaining postmasters. There seems to have been still some feeling as to the Crown monopoly, for we find in 1649 the Common Council of London setting up a post in competition with that of Parliament, but the Commons, though they had loudly denounced the formation of the Crown monopoly, now promptly put down this infringement of their own monopoly, and from this time the carriage of letters has remained in the hands of the Government.

During Cromwell's administration the Post Office underwent material changes, the establishment of posts being regarded by the Government of that day as "the best means to discover and prevent many dangerous and wicked designs against the Commonwealth." The postal arrangements made under Cromwell's rule were confirmed at the Restoration by the Act 12 Carl. II., c. 35, which Act is the first strictly legal authority for the establishment of a Post Office, and in consequence is known as its charter.

In Scotland postal matters fared badly until 1635, when a system for the conveyance of letters from London to Edinburgh was established, though without provision being made for internal posts. During the last half of the 17th century, several such posts were established on the principal lines of road, but it was not until the reign of William III. that these arrangements received legislative sanction, when in 1695 the Scotch Parliament passed an Act for the general establishment of a letter post.

One of the most important epochs in postal history is undoubtedly the establishment of a London district post. It was in the year 1683 that one Robert Murray, an upholsterer, being dissatisfied with the existing arrangements, established in London a penny post on his own account, and at great expense. The scheme, which was simple enough in its details, worked very well, and became a great success, both on the public side and that of the proprietor. It subsequently passed into the hands of a William Dockwra,

B

a name that is now well-known in the annals of
Post Office history, and it is a curious commentary on
the spirit of that age that the success of the system
caused it to be denounced by the Ultra-Protestant
party, as a contrivance of the Jesuits, it being alleged
that if the bags were examined they would be found
full of Popish plots.   The arrangements were not
wanting in liberality, as may be gathered from the
fact that all letters or parcels not exceeding a *pound*
in weight, or any sum of money not exceeding £10
in value, or parcel not worth more that £10 could be
conveyed at a cost of one penny ; or within a radius
of ten miles from a given centre, for the charge of
twopence.   Several district offices, too, were opened
in various parts of London, and receiving-houses
were freely established in all the leading thorough-
fares.   Stowe, the Metropolitan antiquarian, in his
"Annals" says that in the windows of the latter offices,
or other prominent places, were large printed placards
intimating, "Penny post letters taken in here."
"Letter carriers," he adds, "gather them each hour,
and take them thence to the grand office in their
respective circuits.   After the said letters and parcels
are duly entered in the books, they are delivered at
stated periods by other carriers."   The number of
deliveries in the city was from six to eight, while
those in the suburbs numbered from three to four.
It will be seen that under this system the London
public were afforded considerable facilities for letter
communication, and it is not surprising therefore that
the undertaking proved a great commercial and
financial success.   Indeed, the profits of the concern
increased to such an extent that they excited the
envy of the Government, who seized the post on the

ground of its being an infringement of the rights of the Crown. Dockwra, however, was afterwards awarded a pension of £200 a-year by way of compensation, and he was subsequently appointed Controller of the system. Such was the commencement of the London District Post, which, until the year 1854 existed as a separate department of the General Post Office.

In 1698 Dockwra was removed from his office on a charge of mismanagement, the charge being contained in a memorial by the officers and messengers of the Penny Post (as the District Post was then called) to the Commissioners of the Treasury. He was charged not only with stopping parcels but also with malversation, with the opening of letters and extracting bills, and with persecuting all the officers except his own creatures.

In 1708 a Mr. Povey attempted the establishment of a Half-penny Post in opposition to the official Penny Post, but, like Dockwra's enterprise, it was suppressed by a law suit.

The whole postal establishment of the country was remodelled in 1710 in the reign of Good Queen Anne, the Statute c. 10 of that reign repealing the Act of Charles II. as well as the Scotch Act of 1695, and this Act remained until 1837 the foundation of that branch of the law. Under its provisions one general Post Office was established for the three kingdoms and the colonies under one Postmaster-General, who was empowered to keep one chief Letter Office in London, one in Edinburgh, and one in Dublin, one in New York, and one in the West Indies. The Irish Post Office, however, became separated from the British Post Office in 1784, by an Irish Act of Parliament, and an independent Postmaster-General for that country was created, but the two offices became re-united under a British Postmaster-General by the Act 1 William IV. c. 8, 1831.

The most important postal event after the passing of the above-mentioned Statute of Anne is undoubtedly the farming of the cross posts in 1720 by Ralph Allen, who bears an honoured name in postal history, and is also celebrated by reason of his being the original of Squire Allworthy in Fielding's " Tom Jones." Allen was Deputy Postmaster of Bath, and in his official capacity had therefore considerable opportunity of observing the imperfect organisation of the existing cross posts. These, indeed, were so few that many districts were totally unprovided with a postal service ; in other cases letters passing between neighbouring towns were carried by circuitous routes, causing serious delays in those days of slow locomotion. Allen readily saw that the extension and re-organisation of these posts would result not only in an improvement to public accommodation, but also to the public revenue, and he was able to induce the Government to grant him a lease of the cross posts for life at an annual rental of £6000. The improvements which he carried out in this branch of the postal service were eminently successful, and resulted in an annual profit to himself of upwards of £12,000, which he enjoyed for forty-four years, spending it mainly in charity and hospitality to men of learning and genius. At his death, in 1764, the system was placed under the control of William Ward, who for a salary of £300 a-year undertook to hand over the profits, amounting to £20,000 a-year, to the Crown. The increase of this branch of the postal service was

very rapid, and in 1799, when the Bye Letter Office
was abolished, and its functions transferred to the
General Post Office, the annual profits amounted to
£200,000, so extraordinary was the increase.

The most prominent name in early Post Office
history is undoubtedly that of John Palmer, who in
1784 effected what is officially described as "one of
the greatest reforms ever made in the Post Office,"
and which was in fact the carriage of the mails by
coach.   Up to that time, as we are told, the mail-bags

AN EARLY MAIL COACH.

had been carried by post-boys on horseback, at an
average speed, including stoppages, of from three to
four miles an hour.   To properly appreciate the state
of things which then existed, it may be well to quote
the account which Palmer gives of the existing system
in the scheme he submitted in 1783 to Mr. Pitt.
"The Post," he says, "at present, instead of being the
swiftest, is almost the slowest, conveyance in the
country ; and though, from the great improvement in
our roads, other carriers have proportionately mended

their speed, the post is as slow as ever. It is likewise very unsafe, as the frequent robberies of it testify ; and to avoid a loss of this nature people generally cut bank bills or bills at sight in two, and send the bills by different posts. The mails are generally intrusted to some idle boy, without character, mounted on a worn-out hack, and who, so far from being able to defend himself or escape from a robber, is much more likely to be in league with him." Mr. Palmer, who, like Allen, hailed from Bath, being the manager of the theatre in that city, had observed that when the tradesmen there were particularly anxious to have a letter conveyed with speed and safety, they were in the habit of enclosing it in a brown paper cover and sending it by the coach, though the charge for such conveyance was much higher than the postage of a letter. His proposal, therefore, was that as far as possible the mail-bags should be sent by the passenger coaches, accompanied by well-armed and trustworthy guards. He also proposed that the mails should be so timed as to arrive in London, and, as far as might be, in other places at the same hour, so that the letters might be delivered all together ; and that they should be despatched from and arrive in London at a time convenient to the public, the mails having hitherto left London at all hours of the night. Obvious as were the advantages of such a plan, it met with considerable opposition in many quarters, but its merits commended themselves to Mr. Pitt, under whose auspices an Act of Parliament was passed authorising its adoption. This was the beginning of the mail coach era, which will be dealt with more fully in a subsequent chapter, as will also the initiation of a systematic delivery of the letters.

A POST OFFICE IN 1790.

The new system proved successful in every respect, the speed of the mails being at once increased from three and a-half to more than six miles an hour, still greater acceleration being subsequently effected. And, although the improvement caused some additions to the rates of postage, it resulted in a great immediate increase of correspondence, as well as of revenue, which advanced steadily for many years afterwards.

It will be seen from the foregoing facts, which have been narrated as briefly as possible, that the postal arrangements of this country down to the close of the eighteenth century, were at best of a crude and irregular character, and it is difficult in these days of immense postal facilities to appreciate the adverse conditions under which correspondence was carried on in the previous century. There then existed but little system or regularity in the despatch and receipt of the mails, and the community in general suffered under disadvantages which, while hard for us to conceive of in the present day, were not perhaps so keenly felt by our forefathers, inasmuch as they had never been accustomed to anything better. The true story and most interesting epoch of postal history really commences with the inauguration of penny postage, and the years immediately preceding that date, for that was the actual beginning of the romance of the British Post Office. We hasten, therefore, to deal with this subject in the next chapter.

CHAPTER II.

PRIOR TO PENNY POSTAGE.

THE boon of penny postage has now so long been enjoyed that it is somewhat difficult to grasp the full importance of that reform. Especially is this the case as regards the younger portion of the community, who have never been accustomed to other than cheap postage. Imagine, if possible, for a moment how it would be now if the dream of penny postage still remained unrealised. Every grade and section of society would be affected. Trade and commerce would be robbed of one of their most important accessories. Thus would the merchant be unable, except at high rates, to post his advices and invoices, the commercial traveller his notices of advent, and the tradesman his circulars and bills, for which last some, perhaps, would be grateful. The legal and medical professions would be affected proportionately, as also would science, art and literature. As for social life generally, the extent to which it would suffer is simply appalling to contemplate. The breakfast-table would be robbed of one of its greatest joys, for is not the budget of letters one of the chief delights of the matutinal meal? Then, not to speak of private correspondence passing between relations, friends and acquaintances, we should have to forego the

26

pleasure of sending Christmas, birthday and all other festive cards. Loving swains, too, would have to place their valentines under the door as of yore, or else would the custom become a dead letter for which the more prosaic would no doubt be thankful. The picture, of course, has its reverse side. For we should not be inundated with circulars, or importuned by begging and charity letters, whilst debtors would enjoy immunity from dunning letters. Editors, too, must sigh for the days of high letter charges that alone could prevent the shoals of manuscripts with which they are wont to be deluged. But penny postage was intended to benefit the million, and this assuredly it has done, for its beneficial effects have reached to the uttermost ends of the earth, and advantageously influenced the whole of civilised humanity.

If we look back some sixty years we shall find a state of society which, so far as the letter post was concerned, was considerably out of condition. The mails, still conveyed for the most part by coach, were dispatched at infrequent intervals, while the deliveries were made with equal uncertainty. The great drawback was, of course, the high charges, which were such as to be almost prohibitive, except in London and one or two of the leading provincial cities, where cheap local posts existed. These charges, which varied according to distance, depended not only upon weight, but also upon the number of enclosures. Thus, a letter weighing less than an ounce, with one enclosure, if for delivery thirty miles out of London, cost 3d., if eighty miles out, 4d., and so on. As showing how the charge according to enclosure operated, a letter with a single enclosure from London to Edinburgh was charged 1s. 1½d.; if double, 2s. 3d.;

and if treble, 3s. 4½d.   Moreover, the charges were not consistently made, for whereas an Edinburgh letter, posted in London, was charged 1s. 1½d., a letter for Louth, which cost the Post Office fifty times as much as the former letter, was only charged 10d.   In London matters were somewhat better, for there existed the " Twopenny Post " which had in 1801 succeeded to the Penny Post of Robert Murray, referred to in the previous chapter.   The limits of this post extended to places not exceeding twelve miles from the General Post Office, St. Martin's le Grand, and this arrangement continued until the time of uniform penny postage.

With the high charges and diversified rates as shown, it may well be imagined that in those days there was but little incentive to letter-writing.   One of the many results of those high and varying charges was the evasion of postage altogether by illicit modes of conveyance, as well as by the abuse of the then existing franking privilege.   In spite of the penal laws then in force, contraband letters were sent in enormous quantities ; so much so that there were carriers who did almost as much business as the Post Office itself.   Indeed, the practice was so general, that leading merchants throughout the country freely availed themselves of such methods.   Some idea of the state to which matters had been carried may be formed when we find a leading journal boldly asserting in relation to the subject that "*fortunately* for trade and commerce, the operation of the Government monopoly is counteracted by the clandestine conveyance of letters."

. Here is an incident which forcibly illustrates the ingenious methods then in vogue for evading postage. The incident is related in connection with a visit of

the poet Coleridge to the Lakes district. Halting at
the door of a wayside inn just as the postman had
delivered a letter to the barmaid, he noticed that after
turning it over and over she returned it to the postman, saying she could not afford to pay the postage,
which was a shilling. This the poet gallantly insisted
on paying, in spite of some resistance on the barmaid's
part, which, of course, seemed quite natural. He was
rather astonished, however, to learn afterwards that
the envelope had told her all she wanted to know.
It seems she and her brother had pre-arranged that a
few hieroglyphics on the cover should convey all that
was wanted to be told, whilst the letter contained no
writing. "We are so poor," added the girl, "that we
have invented this manner of corresponding and
franking our letters."

Newspapers, which in those days passed free within
a stated period through the post, the stamp-duty
covering the postage, were also a favourite vehicle for
letter-smuggling. Invisible ink, too, was often used
for inditing messages on the newspapers themselves,
while short communications were frequently conveyed
in the address. For example, "Mr. V. W. Smith"
intimated by the letters "V. W." that the sender was
very well in health. Letter-smuggling was, indeed,
carried on to an extent that is hardly credible. Thus,
it was stated by many Manchester merchants, including Mr. Cobden, in evidence before the Post Office
Inquiry Committee appointed in 1838, that four-fifths
of the letters written in that town did not pass through
the Post Office. A carrier in Scotland confessed to
having carried sixty letters daily for a number of
years, and knew of others who carried five hundred
daily. A Glasgow publisher and bookseller said he

sent and received fifty letters or circulars, and added that he was not caught until he had sent twenty thousand letters otherwise than through the post!

But the most favoured way of evading the postage duties was undoubtedly the franking privilege enjoyed by both Houses of Parliament. Originally introduced, no doubt, to enable members to correspond with their constituents, the system, as is not surprising, perhaps, speedily became very much abused, and many were the dodges and tricks resorted to in order to obtain the necessary useful frank. It was common for letters to be delayed until a frank could be obtained. The readers of such books as Cowper's "Life and Letters" and Moore's "Correspondence" will find that the efforts to obtain franks or carriage for their MSS. or proofs occasioned these poets frequent uneasiness, and lost them much time. In assize towns people eagerly awaited the arrival of the judge to get their letters franked by him, and peers and members of the House of Commons were assailed at every opportunity, and pestered out of their very lives for their signatures, which they seem to have given away wholesale. An official in a provincial Post Office carried on a regular correspondence with his brother in Ireland through the intervention of a noble lord in London, to whom the letters from both directions were sent under cover, and who good-naturedly affixed his signature to them and sent them on their way rejoicing. This from a Post Office official!

The abuse of the franking privilege was by no means, however, confined to letters, and at one time, indeed, all sorts of curious packages passed free under the system. Dogs, a cow, parcels of lace, bales of stockings, boxes of medicine, flitches of bacon are among the articles that were so sent. But we learn of worse even than this, for we read of the frank being used to cover the postage of "two maid-servants going as laundresses to my Lord Ambassador Methuen." Or, again, "Dr. Crichton carrying with him a cow and divers necessaries;" "fifteen couples of hounds going to the king of the Romans;" and "three suits of *cloaths* for some nobleman's lady at the Court of Portugal."

The evil, it will be seen, was indeed a serious one, and it is appalling to think what amount of revenue was lost thereby. When the control of the packet service was taken away from the Post Office, the franking privilege ceased to be abused in this manner, but it still continued in regard to letters. Of course the abuse was not permitted to go on altogether unheeded, and amongst other means adopted to cure the evil, Parliament enacted that the whole address of the letter should be in the handwriting of the member, his signature to be also appended. This measure appears, however, to have been only partially successful, and it was subsequently ordered that all franks should be dated, the month to be written in full, and the letters to be posted on the day they bore date. Amongst other repressive measures it was enacted that franked letters were only to carry one ounce, and were only to pass free when posted within twenty miles of the place where the member concerned was on that or the preceding day. Also the number allowed to be sent by one person in one day was restricted to ten, and to fifteen received. Notwithstanding these restrictions, the number of franked letters increased enormously down to the very date of penny postage, and the abuses with them, but no further statutory change was made. Members throughout the country would sign huge packets of covers at one time and distribute them amongst their friends and adherents. Sometimes they even sold them, and servants have been known to receive them in lieu of wages, they selling them again in the ordinary way of business. We are told that in 1838, just prior to the introduction of penny postage, the number of franks which actually passed through the Post Office was estimated at seven millions, and had they been liable to regular charge according to weight they would have added nearly a *million* sterling to the postal revenue of that year!

The following extract from a letter written by the poet Cowper to the Rev. W. Unwin, respecting the restrictions on franking, is a curious commentary on the morality of the age. "The privilege of franking," he writes, "having been so cropped, I know not in what manner I and my bookseller are to settle the conveyance of proof sheets hither and back again. They must travel, I imagine, by coach, a large quantity of them at a time; for, like other authors, I find myself under a poetical necessity of being frugal."

It will be seen, then, that the high postage rates with their attendant abuses had made the time ripe for some sweeping reform. The Post Office had, of course, progressed in some respects, but it, or perhaps more strictly speaking the Treasury, would not budge in the matter of charges. In 1837 the average general postage was estimated at 9½d. per letter, or 8¾d. excluding foreign letters. The postage of a letter from London to Edinburgh was, in the reign of Queen Anne, less than half the amount charged at the accession of Queen Victoria. It is hardly surprising to learn, therefore, that these high rates had the effect of making the Post Office revenue remain stationary for nearly twenty years. Of course it is not to be understood that the Post Office and its abuses at this time suffered an immunity from public criticism, and chief among the champions of Post Office reform was Mr. Wallace of Kelly, the member for Greenock, who was fierce in his denunciation of the existing postal abuses and irregularities. His frequent motions, while they were indeed the means of drawing public attention to the desirability of postal reform, drew upon him the wrath of many Ministers and others. "I never," impatiently exclaimed Lord William Lennox in the House of Commons on one occasion, "take up my papers in the morning that I do not find the name of the honourable member for Greenock there with some motion for inquiry with respect to the Post Office. I wish to God that the honourable member would bring forward that inquiry at once in some tangible shape, instead of indulging in vague generalities and mere declamation." Nevertheless, in spite of the animosity displayed against him, there is no doubt that Mr. Wallace of Kelly paved the way for Rowland Hill and the reform of penny postage. He was indeed one of the trusty friends whom the latter took into council, and Rowland Hill generously acknowledged the assistance he received from Mr. Wallace. "He gave me," states Hill, "the advantage of his position, and laboured through three anxious years to promote my views as earnestly as if they had been his own."

C

CHAPTER III.

ROWLAND HILL AND PENNY POSTAGE.

THE year 1840 will ever be remembered as the great land-mark in Post Office history, that being the date of the accomplishment of Rowland Hill's grand idea of penny postage, a social reform which has unquestionably spread its beneficial influence over every country where a postal system exists. Born in 1795 at Kidderminster, Rowland Hill was considerably past middle age before he entertained any idea of practising his reforming hand on the Post Office. He passed a busy existence till then, chiefly as a schoolmaster, in which capacity he had indulged in many schemes, scholastic and otherwise, with more or less success. His earliest years were, indeed, spent in the stern school of poverty, for his father, of whom it was said "he had every sense but common-sense," appears to have been peculiarly unsuccessful. The family lived in an old farmhouse called Horsehills, at a very low rent, on account of its "being haunted," and bread, butter and lettuces formed not an uncommon dinner with them. One dares hardly think how they passed through such years as 1800 when the dearth was so terrible that men could scarcely for many a year talk of it without a shudder. The elder Hill at the

34

age of forty left trade, for which he was little fitted, and became a schoolmaster, and Rowland's constant association with his father's school gave him almost unconsciously general scholastic knowledge.   He continued his scholastic life down to the year 1833, and at Bruce Castle, Tottenham, his labours in that

BIRTHPLACE OF SIR ROWLAND HILL, AT KIDDERMINSTER.

direction came to an end.   It was about this time that a commission was formed for colonising South Australia, and through his friend Edward Gibbon Wakefield, Rowland Hill was appointed its secretary, a post he held for four years.   It was in 1835, while fulfilling these duties, that he turned his attention earnestly and seriously to the matter of Post Office reform. His thoughts were directed to the subject by the large surplus shown in the national revenue of that year, and his method was as follows.

The basis from which he started was, that it was important in reducing taxation to select that tax the reduction of which would afford a maximum of relief to the public with a minimum of injury to the public revenue. The test he adopted was to examine each tax as to whether its productiveness had kept pace with the increase and prosperity of the nation. The tax that proved most defective under this test was the one required, and that upon the transmission of letters was brought into bad pre-eminence. The absolute postal revenue during the previous twenty years (1815–1835) had diminished, and this notwithstanding that the population had increased ; so that even from a financial point of view the postal rates were injuriously high. But the most serious evil these rates inflicted upon the public was "the obstruction it raised to the moral and intellectual progress of the people." The best possible manner of redressing the evil was of course what Mr. Hill sought. As, however, the only sources of information open to him were the Blue Books, the work was somewhat difficult.

Of this raw material about half-a-hundredweight was furnished him by Mr. Wallace of Kelly, M.P. for Greenock, of whom mention has already been made. The starting-point of course was the simple idea that the postage rates must be reduced, but Hill had not gone far before he arrived at the conclusion that such a reduction might be carried to a considerable extent. It was therefore a question "how far the total reduction might safely be carried." To answer this a systematic study, analysis, and comparison were necessary.

This examination brought out the fact that the practice which then existed of regulating the amount of postage according to the distance an inland letter was conveyed had no foundation in principle. It appeared that the difference in cost of transit in the delivery of a letter (say) at a mile from the posting-place, and of one posted in London and delivered in Edinburgh was an insignificant fraction of a farthing. The conclusion of course was that the rates of postage should be irrespective of distance ; and it was this discovery that formed the basis of the great plan of penny postage. Another conclusion Mr. Hill arrived at was that to make a fixed charge below a given weight instead of charging according to the number of sheets or scraps of paper enclosed would abolish an unjust as well as an inconvenient mode of letter taxation. A third and hardly less important point was how to devise a means of prepayment of letters, acceptable to the public, so as to lessen the cost of delivering letters from house to house. It was clear that the prevailing practice of throwing the postage on the recipients was an improper one, while it was also a burden on the Post Office employés. Considerable difficulty was experienced in arriving at a feasible method of providing for a means of prepayment of postage. The payment of money over the counter was at first thought of, but it was subsequently considered that the purposes of the Post Office and the public would be best served by the use of stamped labels.

The satisfactory settlement of the above-mentioned

points led Rowland Hill to decide that a uniform penny postal rate for inland letters below half-an-ounce in weight could wisely be introduced, and when he published the conclusions he had arrived at, in January, 1837, in his famous pamphlet on "Post Office Reform: Its Importance and Practicability," it will be readily understood what an immense sensation his astounding propositions caused throughout the country. The pamphlet, headed "Private and Confidential," was circulated amongst all the members of the Government, and the first result was a summons to wait upon the Chancellor of the Exchequer, who received Hill courteously and listened attentively to his representations. It may be of interest to give in his own words the conclusions he had arrived at.

"First, that the number of letters passing through the post would be greatly increased by the disuse of franks and abandonment of illicit conveyance; by the breaking up of one long letter into several shorter ones; by the use of many circulars hitherto withheld; and, lastly, by an enormous enlargement of the class of letter writers.

"Further, that, supposing the public, according to its practice in other cases, only to expend as much in postage as before, the loss to the net revenue would be but small; and, again, that such loss, even if large, would be more than compensated by the powerful stimulus given by low postage to the productive power of the country, and the consequent increase of revenue in other departments.

"Finally, that while the risk to the Post Office revenue was comparatively small, and the chance of eventual gain not inconsiderable, and while the beneficial effect on the general revenue was little less than certain, the adoption of my plan would certainly confer a most important, manifest, and acceptable benefit on the country."

The Government did not seem inclined to make any experiment, strongly as these views were represented, and Hill therefore deemed it necessary to appeal directly to public opinion by a re-issue of his pamphlet in a public form under the title of "Post Office Reform, Second Edition." Within the year of publication, a third edition had been called for, and the support of the press was almost universal. Public bodies took the matter up, and as may be imagined the plan found ready favour with the mercantile world. Even the more thoughtful could not deny that, although novel in character, the whole scheme bore traces of the greatest care and attention. Indeed, the public soon began to clamour, and in the course of six days 215 petitions in favour of uniform penny postage were presented to Parliament. During the session of 1839, the number of petitions was upwards of 2000, and the appended signatures about a quarter of a million. Twenty-five London journals and eighty-seven provincial papers supported the scheme, while even abroad the question excited considerable attention. *The Times*, in March, 1839, thus described the situation :—" On a review of the public feeling which it (penny postage) has called forth from men of all parties, sects, and conditions of life, it may well be termed the cause of the whole people of the United Kingdom against the small coterie of place-holders in St. Martin's le Grand and its dependencies." Lord Brougham, with his usual clear-sighted vision, declared that nothing he had heard had in the least

degree shaken his opinion as to the utility and feasi-
bility of the plans. Complaints, too, as to the high
postage rates, which previously had never been made,
flowed in after the publication of Mr. Hill's pamphlet.
A mercantile committee was also formed, which,
during all the time of the agitation, actively spread
information of the progress of the plan with a view to
rouse the public to a sense of its importance. Hand-
bills, fly sheets, and pictorial illustrations were freely
distributed. One print took a dramatic form, representing "A scene at Windsor Castle," in which the
Queen, being in the Council Chamber, is made to say:
"Mothers pawning their clothes to pay the postage of
a child's letter! Every subject studying how to evade
the postage without caring for the law." (To Lord
Melbourne): "I trust, my lord, you have commanded
the attendance of the Postmaster-General and Mr.
Rowland Hill, as I directed, in order that I may hear
the reasons of both about this universal Penny
Postage plan, which appears to me likely to remove
all these great evils." After the interview takes place
the Queen is made to record the opinion that the
plan "would confer a great boon on the poorer classes
of my subjects, and would be the greatest benefit to
religion, morals, to general knowledge, and to trade."
This *jeu d'esprit*, published by the London committee,
was circulated by thousands, and brought the burning
question home in an attractive form to the masses of
the nation.

On the other hand, Rowland Hill's scheme met
with the bitterest opposition, not only from the
Government and the Opposition, but also from
many other quarters. The Postmaster - General
characterised the proposals as the "most extrava-

gant of all the wild and visionary schemes" he had ever heard of. Six months later, when he had given the subject more attention, he endorsed this statement, being "even still more firmly of the same opinion." On a subsequent occasion, this same Postmaster-General, Lord Lichfield, contended that the mails would have to carry twelve times as much in weight as before, and therefore the charge would be twelve times the amount then paid. "The walls of the Post Office," he exclaimed, "would burst ; the whole area in which the building stands would not be large enough to receive the clerks and letters !" Mr. Godby, of the Irish Post Office, said : " He did not think any human being would ever live to see such an increase of letters as would make up the loss by the proposed reductions." Had he lived till now, assuredly he would have been fully convinced.

The agitation as to the Penny Postage scheme lasted for two years, and with such vehemence that the period has become an epoch in the history of the country. The end is soon told ; for an agitation which shook the nation to its core, and was felt from end to end of the kingdom, could have but one conclusion, and that a successful one. A Parliamentary Committee was appointed to inquire into the whole matter ; and, after a session of sixty-three days, reported in favour of Penny Postage. That was in August, 1838. On the 5th of July in the following year, the Chancellor of the Exchequer, in bringing forward his Budget, formally proposed the experiment of Penny Postage. The resolution was agreed to without a division, and, some days later, the Bill on the subject was introduced into the House of Commons. It passed through both Houses of Parliament without a division, and became law on the 17th of August, 1839. On the 12th of November of that year, the Treasury issued a minute authorising a uniform rate of fourpence for inland letters. This, however, was merely a temporary measure, in which Rowland Hill concurred, and was resorted to chiefly to accustom the Post Office clerks to a uniform rate, and the system of charging by weight. The full measure of the Penny Postage scheme was accomplished a few months later, when, on the 10th of January, 1840, the uniform rate of One Penny for letters not exceeding half-an-ounce in weight was officially introduced.

Thus was the battle won, and Rowland Hill was the hero of the day. Congratulations poured in, and the inhabitants of Wolverhampton testified their high sense of his services as the " Founder and able Advocate of the Plan of Universal Penny Postage—A.D. 1839," by the presentation of a handsome silver candelabrum. It, of course, became a question what the Government intended doing for Hill, for it was evident he must be recompensed and receive a Crown appointment. At first he was engaged temporarily for a term of two years at the Treasury, at a salary of £1500 a-year, without any claim to permanent employment at the end of that period. Although he did good work during this engagement, which was extended to another year, he yet found it difficult to develop his original plan in its entirety. On the accession of the Conservatives, who had opposed the Penny Postage plan, Hill lost his place at the Treasury. It was not long, however, before he obtained a Directorship, and, shortly afterwards, the Chairmanship, of the Brighton Railway Company.

He remained in this capacity for four years, and effected such reforms in this railway system that the property rose considerably in value.

Meanwhile, a Select Committee was appointed by the House of Commons to inquire into the state of the Post Office, and Hill himself had published a pamphlet — "The State and Prospects of Penny Postage." In 1846, the Liberals had such strong hopes of a speedy return to power that Rowland Hill resigned his Chairmanship of the Brighton Railway Company, and a large annual income (in one year alone he made £6000), for a comparatively insignificant Government appointment. These hopes were realised, for, on the 29th of June, the Conservative Ministry, with Sir Robert Peel at its head, resigned. Soon afterwards, Hill was permanently appointed Secretary to the Postmaster-General at a salary of £1200, but his power was still greatly restricted, owing to the opposition of the then Secretary of the Post Office and the leading officials of that department. There can be no doubt that the Government would have appointed Hill to be sole Secretary to the Post Office had that post been vacant, but the then holder of the office was too young a man to pension, and there was no suitable position to which he could at that time be transferred. In 1854, however, a seat at the Board of Audit was found for the Chief Secretary, and the posts of Secretary to the Post Office and Secretary to the Postmaster-General were consolidated in the person of Rowland Hill, an appointment fully endorsed by the public.

In smooth waters at last, Mr. Hill continued for ten years at the great work of his life. The mail services at one time would engage his attention ; he instituted the "Limited Mail," and his son invented the expedient for trains delivering and receiving the mail bags at certain places without the necessity for stopping. At another time the system of Foreign and Colonial postage claimed his consideration, or the Money Order Office, or the rectification of accounts. On three occasions he was threatened with assassination on account of some alleged grievance on the part of the letter-carriers.

On the 29th of February, 1864, Rowland Hill resigned his appointment at the Post Office in consequence of failing health. He was awarded his full salary of £2000 a-year for life. On the 11th of June, 1864, Lord Palmerston, as Prime Minister, in the House of Commons, brought up a message from the Queen recommending the House to concur in enabling her to grant the author of Penny Postage the sum of £20,000 in consideration of his eminent services. Lord Palmerston, in moving the grant of this sum, testified to the "great genius, sagacity, perseverance, and industry, and to the services rendered by Sir Rowland Hill to this and to other countries." It should be mentioned that, in 1860, the distinction of Knight Commander of the Bath had been conferred by Her Majesty on Rowland Hill.

The public, too, were anxious to show honour to Sir Rowland, and as early as 1846 a national testimonial of £13,000 had been subscribed and presented to him at Blackwall. In 1860 he was elected a member of the Royal Society, on the recommendation of the Duke of Argyll and Sir Robert Murchison (Astronomer-Royal), and a year later he was admitted to that inner circle, the Royal Society Club. The University of Oxford conferred on him the honorary degree of D.C.L., and in 1879 the City of London granted him its freedom. He was an old man then, however, and only lived a few months to enjoy this civic honour, for he died on the 27th of August, 1879. The nation awarded him the honour of a resting-place in Westminster Abbey. "The funeral was not," writes a mourner who was present, "a State ceremonial—it was a people's payment of honour. There was not grief ; but there was a solemn sense of recognition of a great deed."

In the character of the author of Penny Postage there was a "rare combination of enthusiasm and practical power." He was confident of success, yet always cautious in procedure. In everything but work he was a most temperate man. He was hot-tempered, but the most upright and truthful of men. The testimony of one who long served under him affords a very good summary of his public character. "Sir Rowland Hill was very generous," he states, "with his own money, and very close with the public money. He would have been more popular had he been generous with the public and close with his own."

It remains to say a few words as to the early results of the system of Penny Postage. These are to be regarded from two points of view—namely, the social and commercial, and the financial. As regards the former aspect, history records that the success of the system, after it had been in operation two years, exceeded even the most sanguine expectations of its most zealous advocates. This, indeed, is at once apparent from the recorded fact that the number of chargeable letters passing through the Post Office increased from 76 millions in 1839, the year immediately preceding the introduction of Penny Postage, to

169 millions in 1840; and the number continued to increase rapidly in each succeeding year.

The influence of the system on commercial enterprise and social life was quite marvellous, as was abundantly testified to before the Parliamentary Committee of 1843. The scheme had almost entirely put an end to breaches of the law, and any illicit correspondence that was still carried on was purely in cases where speed was a consideration. Even the smallest commercial transactions were now arranged through the post. The use of small money orders became constant, the business of the Money Order Office having increased almost *twenty-fold*, owing to the reduced postage rates of 1840, and the reduction of money order commission in the same year. " These orders," it was stated, " are generally acknowledged. Printers send their proofs without hesitation ; the commercial traveller writes regularly to his principal, and is enabled for the first time to advise his customers of his approach ; private individuals and public institutions distribute widely their circulars and their accounts of proceedings to every part of the land."

A mass of correspondence flowed in upon Mr. Hill between 1840 and 1842—which he read to the Select Committee—testifying to the great benefits his plan had conferred. Tradesmen wrote saying how their business had increased. One large merchant now sent the whole of his invoices by post ; another increased his " prices current " by 10,000 per annum. A large and well-known firm of carriers despatched by post eight times the number of letters posted in 1839 ; whilst, had the letters been chargeable according to single sheets, they would have numbered

720,000 in 1842 from this one firm, as against 30,000 in 1839. Mr. Charles Knight, the London publisher, said that the Penny Postage stimulated every branch of his trade, and brought country booksellers into almost daily communication with the London houses. Mr. Bagster, the publisher of a Polyglot Bible in twenty-four languages, stated to Mr. Hill that the revision he was then making, as it was passing through the press, would have cost him £1500 in postage alone under the old system, and that the Bible could not have been printed but for the Penny Post. Secretaries of benevolent and literary societies, and the conductors of educational establishments, also testified to the extreme usefulness of Penny Postage in their own different connections. The Honorary Secretary of the Parker Society said that but for Penny Postage the Society would never have come into existence. One of the principal advocates for the repeal of the Corn Laws subsequently gave it as his opinion that their objects had been achieved *two years earlier* than would otherwise have been the case, in consequence of Rowland Hill's Postal reform.

The social advantages of Penny Postage to the masses were not less marked. It was due wholly to that system that the late Professor Hounslow, when Rector of Hitcham, was able to arrange a scheme of co-operation for advancing among the landed interest of the county the progress of agricultural science. The mere suggestion, he says, of such a thing involved him in a correspondence he could not have sustained but for the Penny Post. Amongst the variety of specimens he was continually receiving and despatching by post, he tells of "three living carnivorous slugs, which arrived safely in a pill-box!"

He adds, "That the Penny Postage is an important addition to the comforts of the poor labourer I can also testify. From my residence in a neighbourhood where scarcely any labourers can read, much less write, I am often employed by them as an amanuensis, and have frequently heard them express their satisfaction at the facility they enjoy of now being able to correspond with their relatives." Miss Harriet Martineau testified to the great benefits her neighbourhood had derived from the Penny Post scheme, while another celebrated writer declared it was a "much wiser and more effective measure than the Prussian system of education," then introduced. "This measure" (Penny Postage) he adds, "will be the great historical distinction of the reign of Victoria. Every mother in the kingdom who has children earning their bread at a distance will lay her head on the pillow at night with a feeling of gratitude for the blessing."

The Shetlanders, we are told, were delighted with Penny Postage, and though the desire of parents to keep their offspring at home is unusually strong in Shetland, yet cheap postage had the effect of reconciling families to the temporary absence of their members, whereby the labour-market of the mainland was thus opened up to the islanders.

Much more could be written, were it necessary, to show how far and wide reaching was the beneficial influence of Rowland Hill's great postal reform. But sufficient has been said to show that all classes and grades of society,—trade and commerce, science, art, and literature, as well as the professions, reaped incalculable benefits from the apparently simple idea of a uniform Penny Post. Especially noticeable was the operation of Penny Postage on the poorer classes. For, as Rowland Hill himself stated before the Statistical Society in 1841, the postman, after 1840, made "long rounds through humble districts where, heretofore, his knock was rarely heard." Joseph Hume, writing in 1848 to Mr. Bancroft, then American Minister at the Court of St. James's, says: " I am not aware of any reform amongst the many which I have promoted during the past forty years, that has had, and will have better results towards the improvement of the country socially, morally, and politically." The experience of subsequent years has surely exemplified the truth of these words.

The second point of view from which the early years of Penny Postage are to be regarded is not so satisfactory, and the result disappointed even Rowland Hill. Of course Hill had looked for a deficiency of postal revenue at first in consequence of the adoption of his plans. But he estimated that the loss in the first year would not exceed £300,000 ; as a matter of fact it was very much more. In 1842 the loss of revenue amounted to as much as £900,000. It has to be borne in mind, however, that while trade was flourishing when the Postage Bill was carried, in the first year of Penny Postage it was exceedingly depressed. Moreover, Rowland Hill's plans were not carried out in their entirety ; and, as he pointed out, much of the financial success of the scheme depended on that being done. On the other hand, we have to remember that if the postal revenue suffered, there was a decided gain to the general revenue of the country. For the reduction of the postage rates meant a reduction of taxation to the community, and thereby money was freed for dis-

bursement in other directions. At first it was the
opinion of the Post Office that the new plan would
not pay its expenses, but a year's experience
exploded that fallacy. And at the end of three
years there were even indications that the gross
postal revenue under the old system would be
reached; and, as a matter of fact, this was accomplished in 1850–51, when the old gross revenue was
passed. Thirteen years later—namely, in 1863, the
old net revenue was reached, and the deficiency
was wiped out. Henceforward the plan of Penny
Postage has continued to be an unqualified success
from every point of view.

CHAPTER IV.

THE CONVEYANCE OF THE MAILS.

IN the present day when a letter posted in London in the evening is delivered, say, in Edinburgh the next morning, it is difficult to realise the tedious delays which attended the conveyance of correspondence in bygone times. The history of our roads and conveyances is to a great extent the history of the Post Office, for of course every improvement in the means of locomotion has had a distinct influence in the acceleration of the mail service. Had it not been for the discovery of the latent powers of steam and the invention of the steam-engine, the Post Office would obviously never have attained to that high standard of speed in the conveyance of our letters of which it now boasts.

In the early days of the postal system, as has already been seen, the mails were carried by mounted messengers, who subsequently became better known as "post-boys." This system of conveyance was, as may be imagined, at best slow and uncertain; yet, inadequate and inefficient as it undoubtedly was, it continued in operation far into the seventeenth century. The system appears to have been very loosely administered, and owing to the illiberality of the department, only what may be considered the scum of both animals and riders could be obtained for the service. If, in addition to this, the accidents of weather, stoppages on the road through swollen rivers, fogs, footpads and highwaymen be taken into account, the slowness and uncertainty of the system can be well understood.   Not only were the post-boys, as one historian tells us, as a rule without discipline, and difficult to control, but they sauntered on the road at pleasure, and were an easy prey to the highwaymen, with which the roads at that period were infested.   They were continually being robbed, for they had not the means, even if they had had the will, to offer opposition.   Moreover, too, it would appear that many of them were encouraged in their irregularities by the gentry, so much so that we hear of one of the postal surveyors complaining to headquarters that gentlemen on the road " do give much money to the riders, whereby they be very subject to get in liquor, *which stopes the males.*"

The rate at which the mails were conveyed by these post-boys was, under the most favourable circumstances, painfully slow.   An historical instance of the rate of speed is that of a letter sent in July, 1566, by Archbishop Parker from Croydon to Sir W. Cecil at Croxton, a distance of about 63 miles, and which took nearly two days to accomplish the journey.   We are told that it was three months before the news of the abdication of James II. of England reached the Orkney Islands, while in the ordinary course of things it took the best part of a week to convey the mails from London to Edinburgh, a letter posted on Saturday in the English metropolis being due in Edinburgh on the following Thursday.   Even the so-called expresses were little quicker than the ordinary posts, if one may judge by the fact that it took, as we are told, an express 36 hours to accomplish a journey of 136 miles which, as the Postmasters-General of the day stated, "was the usual rate of expresses."

But, unsatisfactory as this means of transit appears to have been, the postal authorities clung to the system, even after waggons and coaches had become a more general mode of conveyance. Not, however, that it can be said that the coaches were much of an improvement as regards speed, for even the "Flying Coach" did not accomplish more than about five miles an hour. It was not until 1784 that a complete reformation of the mail service was effected through the agency of Mr. Palmer, the Bath theatre manager, to whom reference has already been made in a previous chapter. It was also part of Mr. Palmer's plan that the mails should be timed at each successive stage, and their departure from the country properly regulated; and that instead of leaving London at all hours of the night, the coaches for the different roads should leave the General Post Office at the same time, thus establishing what was for many years one of the city sights to the stranger within the gates of London.

It is not surprising to learn that the sweeping reforms in the mail service put forward by Palmer met with anything but a friendly reception by the Post Office authorities, who, indeed, vehemently opposed the proposed changes as being not only "impracticable, but dangerous to commerce and the revenue." The postal system, as it then existed, was considered by the leading officials to be "almost as perfect as it can be, without exhausting the revenue arising therefrom." They further predicted that any such plan as Palmer's "would fling the commercial correspondence of the country into the utmost confusion, and justly raise such a clamour as the Postmaster-General would not be able to appease." One official, while more moderate in his opposition than the others, still gave it as his opinion, "that the more Mr. Palmer's plan was considered, the greater number of difficulties and objections started to its ever being carried completely into execution."

These are only a few of the objections raised by the authorities to Mr. Palmer's scheme, but they are sufficient to show how strenuously it was opposed.

Fortunately, however, the plan recommended itself to the favour of Mr. Pitt, who had just at that time assumed the reins of government as well as holding the post of Chancellor of Exchequer. Pitt, who was remarkable for his clearness of vision, at once perceived that the plan was not only practicable, but would also prove to be profitable, and determined that in spite of all opposition it should be adopted. The Lords of the Treasury forthwith decreed that it should be tried, and on the 24th of July, 1784, Mr. Anthony Todd, the Post Office Secretary, issued the following notice, which may be read with interest at the present time :—

"His Majesty's Postmasters-General, being inclined to make an experiment for the more expeditious conveyance of mails of letters by stage-coaches, machines, etc., have been pleased to offer that a trial shall be made upon the road between London and Bristol, to commence at each place on Monday, the 2nd of August next." A list of places to which letters can be sent by the mail coaches follows, and the document concludes : "All persons are therefore to take notice, that the letters put into any receiving-

house before six of the evening, or seven at this chief
office, will be forwarded by these new conveyances ;
all others for the said post towns and their districts
put in afterwards, or given to the bell men, must
remain until the following post at the same hour of
seven." Although thus advertised to commence

ANTHONY TODD, ESQ.
(*From a Photograph by A. L. Tyler.*)

running on the 2nd of August, the coaches did not
actually start till the 8th of that month, and the journey between London and Bristol was accomplished in
fifteen hours. Complete success seems at once to
have attended the trial, for, notwithstanding a slight
increase in the rates of postage—an addition of a

penny to each charge—the number of letters sent
was very considerably augmented. So greatly
appreciated was the improvement that the munici-
palities of many of the largest towns applied forthwith for coaches, which were mostly granted, and
started at the rate of six miles an hour, which speed
was subsequently increased to ten miles an hour.

Meanwhile, Mr. Palmer had been appointed Con-
troller-General at the Post Office. He appears to
have performed his duties with great ability, but
his task must have been an arduous one, seeing that
the Post Office opposition continued even after the
plan had been so successfully introduced. Not only
did a marked acceleration of speed result from the
change, but also a large increase in correspondence
and revenue. In the first year of the new system the
net revenue of the Post Office was £250,000. Thirty
years later it had attained to £1,500,000. Of course
there were other obvious causes for so great an
increase, but the primary cause was without doubt
the greater speed, security, and punctuality which the
new plan insured.

The improvement in the mail service was, of course,
accompanied by other advantages, such as the increase in the number of deliveries at various places.
The number of mails between some of the largest
towns was, for example, increased, while no less than
380 towns now had a daily delivery where previously
they had had only three in the week. All this
increase of work had a noticeable effect on the London
establishment, and one writer of the time describes the
"immense number of letters despatched nightly from
hence," as "exciting sensations of astonishment in
the mind of the bystander that can only be exceeded

by the rapidity and accuracy with which every part of
the duty is managed." We are told that in 1800 the
staff at the General Post Office had increased quite
twofold in every one of its departments, there being
at the time 18 principal staff appointments, 62 clerks,
26 messengers, 130 inland letter-carriers, 30 super-
numeraries, and 28 foreign letter carriers.

Notwithstanding the great success that his reform
met with, Palmer, like previous reformers, fell a victim
to internal official squabbles, and in 1792 was suspended from his functions, an allowance of £3000
a-year being made to him in lieu thereof. This sum
was much below what he was entitled to under his
agreement, and, after unsuccessfully memorialising
the Treasury against the arrangement, he laid his
case before Parliament, and in 1813, after a struggle
of many years, received a grant out of the public
funds of £50,000.

From the end of last century down to the advent
of the railways, the mail-coach system was an
institution of the country, and with Mr. Macadam's
improved system of road-making their speed became
greatly accelerated. The speed increased to ten
miles an hour and even more, until, in the case of
the Devonport mail, the journey from London of
216 miles was punctually performed, including stoppages, in twenty-one hours and fourteen minutes.

The number of four-horse mail-coaches which ran
in England in 1836, just prior to the general use of the
railways for the conveyance of the mails, was 54, in
addition to 49 of two horses. In Scotland the
number of four-horse coaches was 10, and in Ireland
30. In the last year of mail-coaches, we are told, the
number which left London every night at eight

o'clock was 27, travelling in the aggregate 5500 miles
before they reached their respective destinations.

The official control of the mail-coaches, it may be
stated, was in the hands of the Superintendent of mail-
coaches, who was located at the General Post Office.
With the disappearance of the mail-coach the postal
service has lost much of its picturesque and romantic
side. The transit of the coach from place to place
was a feature in the daily life of the inhabitants, and
was attended by a host of interesting little incidents.

A WEST COUNTRY MAIL-COACH AND CART STARTING FROM
PICCADILLY, 1828.

Famous amongst the coaches was the "Age," which
ran to Brighton, with a baronet for a driver and a
liveried guard, and which has been portrayed in
living colours by Herring. There was also the
"Beaufort," driven by the Marquis of Worcester;
while the Brighton day mail was driven by the
Hon. Fred. Jerningham, son of Lord Stafford.

So attractive does the position appear to have been
that we find it was in many cases filled by aristocratic
drivers, who, we are told, "pocketed their tips with

as much readiness and relish as would the poorest of their congeners." Though we do not hear of any such aristocratic mail-guards, the position was, in point of fact, superior to that of the driver. He was always clothed in the royal livery, as the badge of his office, and his duties were both important and onerous, and sometimes hazardous. These guards were on duty twelve hours at a stretch, and when breakages or overturnings, or stoppages through flood or snowstorms occurred, they had many hardships to contend with. Their pay from the Post Office was only nominal, but the post was lucrative enough owing to the regular perquisites they received ; while in many cases they were intrusted with commissions of great importance, for which, no doubt, they were well paid. Many are the stories that are related of the hardihood and fidelity displayed by the old mail-guards in the discharge of their responsible work, and there can be no doubt that in the olden days the Post Office owed much to their perseverance and devotion to duty.

The old mail-coach in times of excitement was regarded with more than ordinary interest, for it was the first harbinger of news. "The mail-coach it was," says De Quincey, "that distributed over the face of the land, like the opening of apocalyptic vials, the heart-shaking news of Trafalgar, of Salamanca, of Vittoria, of Waterloo." The news of any great victory was proclaimed throughout the journey by the mail-coach being dressed in laurels and flowers, oak leaves and ribbons. "Five years of life," writes one who frequently rode the coaches between 1805 and 1815, "it was worth paying down for the privilege of an outside place on a mail-coach when

carrying down the first tidings of any such event."
Miss Martineau relates that during the trial of Queen
Caroline, "all along the line of mails, crowds stood
waiting in the burning sunshine for news of the trial,
which was shouted out to them as the coach passed."
News now-a-days is, of course, disseminated with
lightning-like speed, but it is doubtful whether it is
received with as keen relish and excitement as of yore.

One of the gayest and liveliest of sights was
the annual procession of mail-coaches on the king's
birthday. "According to custom," says Hone in his
"Everyday Book" for 1822, "the mail-coaches went
in procession from Millbank to Lombard Street.
About twelve o'clock the horses belonging to the
different mails, with entire new harness, and the postmen and postboys, on horseback, arrayed in scarlet
coats and jackets, go to Millbank and there dine;
from thence the procession, being rearranged, begins
to march about five o'clock in the afternoon, headed
by the General Post, then letter-carriers on horseback. The coaches follow filled with the wives and
children, friends and relations of the guards and
coachmen; while the postboys, sounding their bugles
and cracking their whips, bring up the rear. From
the commencement of the procession, the bells of the
neighbouring churches ring out merrily, and continue
their rejoicing peals till it arrives at the Post Office
again, from whence the coaches depart to the
different parts of the country." This procession
took place each year until the disappearance of
the coaches from the road altogether, and, as may
be imagined, was an attractive sight to large numbers
of spectators.

In 1830, on the opening of the Liverpool and

Manchester Railway, the mails were for the first time conveyed by rail, and this may be said to have been the first nail in the coffin of the mail-coaches. As speed is the vital requirement of the mail service, it naturally followed that as the railways grew, their influence should be paramount in the Post Office, and it was only a matter of a few years before they absorbed the whole of the mails. Living in the present age in the full enjoyment of cheap communication, one can readily understand how indissoluble the link between railways and the Post Office soon became, and it is not too much to say, perhaps, that but for the railways, there had been no uniform Penny Postage. Not only was it a question of acceleration of speed, but the accommodation which the railways afforded was also the means of saving time, as it was soon found possible to do much of the letter sorting *en route*. Hence the origin of the Travelling Post Office.

The Travelling Post Office, or T.P.O. as it is frequently called, is a prominent feature, and perhaps one of the most useful in the machinery of the Post Office. The Post Office vans attached to the mail trains must be familiar objects to the ordinary traveller, and it is in such vans, fitted up in all respects as ordinary sorting offices, with sorting tables and pigeon-holes, and plentifully supplied with mail-bags, string, sealing wax, etc., that the work of sorting goes on while the train is passing from place to place. The great advantage of this system is of course the immense saving of time, for the work which would have to be done either before departure or after arrival, is performed whilst the train is in transit, and in this manner correspondence is collected and dis-

posed of at all points along the route, which otherwise
might have to pass through some intermediate town,
suffering delay through detention for a subsequent
means of conveyance.

The first Travelling Post Office was established
on the 1st of July, 1837, on the Grand Junction
Railway between Liverpool and Birmingham, and
on the completion of the railway to the metropolis
in July, 1838, the T.P.O. began to run throughout between London and Liverpool. The speed, we
are told, was then a gentle twenty miles an hour, as
even at a somewhat later period, when the railway
northward had been completed as far as Lancaster,
the mail train took eleven and a-half hours to perform
the journey from London to Lancaster, a distance of
241 miles. Now, when the mail to the north has
travelled eleven hours and a-half it is pulling up at
Forfar, a distance of 471 miles from London.

Travelling Post Offices are attached to numerous
mail trains on all the principal lines, those under the
control of the London Postal service running in the
aggregate about three millions of miles annually over
the chief railway systems of Great Britain. The most
important are probably the "London and North-
Western, and Caledonian," running between London
and Aberdeen, on which 1,800,000 miles, or three-fifths
of the total distance traversed by the mail carriages are
run ; the "Midland and North-Eastern" lines, carrying the mails between Newcastle and Bristol, on which
270,000 miles are run ; and the Great Western Railway, on which 300,000 miles are run. The total
number of letters, etc., dealt with by Travelling Post
Offices is over 210,000,000, besides more than 4,000,000
parcels.

As may be imagined, the work of sorting the letters, etc., in the travelling vans is carried on under considerable difficulties, and is performed for the most part at night. The terms of duty are very broken and irregular, and the sorters employed have many hardships to endure, especially in the winter months. Nevertheless, we learn that there is not a greater amount of sickness amongst this class of

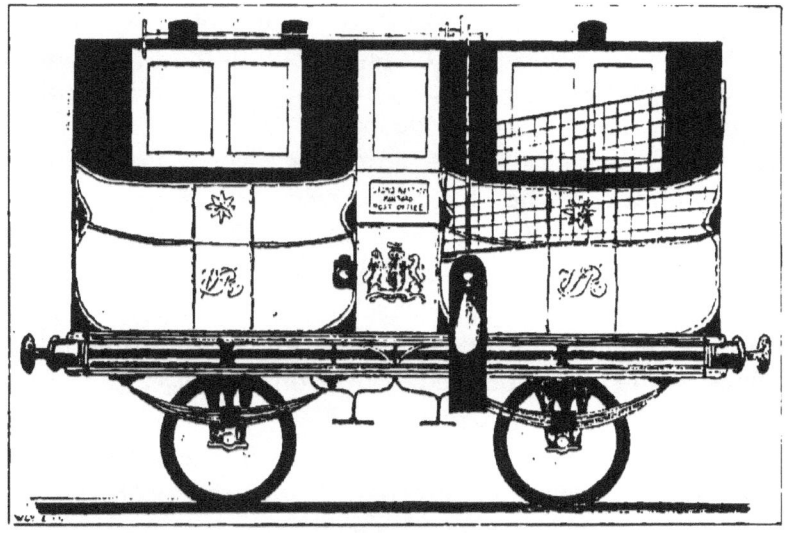

AN EARLY POSTAL VAN.
(*By permission of Messrs. Eyre & Spottiswoode and Messrs. Harmsworth, from "Sixty Years a Queen."*)

sorters than amongst the sorters engaged in the general offices, and many of the men who have travelled 100 miles a-day (Sundays included) for years have stated that they found themselves better for the change from stationary work.

A very important, as well as most useful adjunct of the Travelling Post Office, is the apparatus for receiving mails into, and leaving mails from, mail-trains travel-

ling at full speed. Mr. Ramsay, formerly an officer
of the General Post Office, is said to have suggested
the machinery for the purpose, but it was Mr. Dicker,
also an officer of the Post Office, who improved the
apparatus and made it fit for general use, in recognition of which he received a grant of £500 from the
Treasury, and was appointed Supervisor of Mail-Bag
Apparatus. Further advantageous changes were
made by Mr. Pearson Hill, only son of Sir Rowland
Hill, while still further improvements have of recent
years been devised by Mr. Garrett, the late Supervisor.

The machinery, which provides for the simul-
taneous receipt and despatch of mail-bags, is
worked from a van adjoining the Travelling
Post Office. The bags received are caught in a
net fixed on one side, which can at the proper time
be extended outwards, while the bags to be despatched
are, having first been securely wrapped up in large
pieces of leather and strapped up as a protection
from injury, suspended on iron arms fixed to
the side of the carriage, and which also can be
extended outwards. The apparatus at the stations is
of course an exact counterpart. On nearing the spot
where the exchange is to be made the nets and arms
are put into position and the bags suspended. Then
as the train dashes through at almost lightning speed,
the station net receives the bag suspended to the train
and the train net that suspended at the station, and
the work of opening and sorting the new arrival of
letters is at once proceeded with. As may be
supposed great alacrity and attention have to be
shown in using the apparatus, for arms and net must
not, for fear of accidents, be extended at any but the
appointed places, and within 200 or 300 yards of

where the exchange has to be made. It may be
imagined that the pouch containing the mail-bag often
sustains a severe blow when the train is travelling at
high speed, and on occasions causes damage to the
contents of the bag when of a fragile nature.   A

POSTAL VAN L.N.W.R.
*By permission of Messrs. Eyre & Spottiswoode, and Messrs. Harmsworth,
from "Sixty Years a Queen."*

bracelet sent by post was once thus damaged, giving
rise to the following humorous note :—" Mr. —— is
sorry to return the bracelet to be repaired.   It came
this morning with the box smashed, the bracelet bent
and one of the cairngorms forced out.   Among the
modern improvements of the Post Office appears to

E

be the introduction of sledge-hammers to stamp with. It would be advisable for Mr. —— to remonstrate with the Postmaster-General," etc.

The total number of apparatus stations in England and Wales, and Scotland is 220, and there are 355 standards and 372 nets erected at these stations for the despatch and receipt of mails. The number of Travelling Post Office carriages to which the apparatus nets, etc., is fixed is 44. 516 exchanges of mails are made daily from station standards into carriage nets, and 530 from the carriage to the station nets. The total number of mail-bags included in these exchanges is about 2000. It rarely happens that a bag is missed or dropped, although it has occasionally happened that a pouch is sent bounding over hedges or over the carriage, whilst pouches have been found at the end of a journey on the carriage roof or hanging on to a buffer. In November, 1884, a pouch discharged from the Midland Travelling Post Office missed its net, got cut up, and its contents, including cheques, a silver watch, and a set of artificial teeth, were scattered along the line as far as Normanton. On an average about 110,000 letters, etc., a-day are exchanged by the apparatus at a normal period, of which about 85,000, or nearly four-fifths, are sorted in the Travelling Post Offices, the remainder being sent direct in bags from one town to another through the Travelling Post Offices unopened.

It may be of interest, in concluding this chapter, to state that the conveyance of the mails by railway costs the Post Office more than one and a-half million pounds annually.

CHAPTER V.

AT SAINT MARTIN'S LE GRAND.

AS everyone knows the great English home of letters is at St. Martin's le Grand, London. Here the General Post Office is now represented by three distinct and palatial edifices, known respectively as the General Post Office " East," "West," and " North." The first is given over entirely to the circulation of letters and parcels, the second to the Telegraph Department, and the last-named, which is a recent erection, houses the large administrative staff. These buildings are in themselves substantial evidence of the immense progress which has been made in Post Office business during the present century.

The first General Post Office, it may be mentioned, was opened in Cloak Lane, near Dowgate Hill, and removed from thence to the Black Swan in Bishopsgate Street. This office was destroyed by the great fire of 1666, and a General Post Office was opened in Covent Garden, which, however, was soon removed to Lombard Street, where it remained until 1829, notwithstanding that the building was for a long time very unsuitable for the growing requirements of the office.

When the building now known as the " G.P.O. East"

was completed in the year last mentioned, it was considered one of the handsomest public buildings in London, having been erected from designs by Sir R. Smirke, in the Grecian-Ionic style, with a straight sky-line. Since then, however, the edifice has become sadly disfigured, the straight sky-line having been spoilt by hideous excrescences, for the stupendous growth of business has entirely set aside the original purposes for

THE SORTING ROOM IN THE GENERAL POST OFFICE, LOMBARD STREET, 1829.
(*From a Photograph by A. L. Tyler.*)

which the building was designed, and the interior has been completely altered so as to provide wholly for the letter circulation department. The Controller of the London Postal Service has his offices here, from which all the operations involved in the receipt and despatch of the metropolitan mails are controlled. The rest of the building is occupied, with few exceptions, with the various sorting rooms, the main or great sorting hall being on the ground floor and occupying nearly the whole area of the building.

The interest in the nightly sorting operations commences outside, where a scene of intense excitement may be witnessed for at least a quarter of an hour before six o'clock each evening. As that hour draws nigh the rush is tremendous, men, women and children hurrying from all directions laden with letters, many with baskets full, others with sacks full. For a short time prior to six o'clock the flap of the counter letter box is raised

THE NEW POST OFFICE—1829.
(From a Photograph by A. L. Tyler.)

so as to admit of the wholesale posting of letters, and into the yawning receptacle missives of all kinds are thrown pell mell. Stories are told of baskets and sacks and all being thrown in, in the excitement of the moment. As the minute hand of the great clock in the portico gradually approaches the hour, the rush becomes more and more intense, until, at the last stroke of the hour, the flap is let down with a sharp, sudden snap, and the tardy stragglers who have come up just one moment too late, find themselves face to face with the big notices just put up by the placid-looking policemen standing hard by, and which indicate the extent of the extra fee required for late letters. It is amusing, sometimes, to watch the efforts of some of the belated letter-posters, who endeavour with well-directed aim to project, with Bellerophon-like swiftness, their letters through the letter-slit so as

OUTSIDE THE GENERAL POST OFFICE AT SIX O'CLOCK.

to over-reach the receiving basket on the other side in the vain hope of thereby evading the extra postage.

With the restoration of normal tranquility outside, commences the real rush of business inside. Through sorts of funnels the letters, etc., come tumbling into the baskets provided for their reception on the inner side of the letter-flaps, and as soon as they are filled,

which is in almost less than no time, they are removed
and replaced by others, when the missives and packets
come once more leaping and dancing in. As may be
imagined, the boys who have to attend to the clearing
of the baskets are well employed until the posting-
hour is past. Taking a bird's-eye view from one of
the galleries of the great sorting hall at St. Martin's

BEHIND THE RECEIVER AT THE GENERAL POST OFFICE
AT SIX O'CLOCK.

le Grand, which is now provided with electric light,
the scene presented to the eye is one huge, confused
mass of letters, bags, baskets, etc. Wherever the
gaze turns it is met by mountains of letters and
packages, and immersed in them appear the dark
forms of hundreds of human beings apparently
struggling frantically to overcome these untold legions.

But chaotic as the scene would seem to be, the business of the evening is being pushed rapidly on with systematic routine and precision, as we shall see on descending to the "floor of the house."

Directly the baskets full of correspondence brought from the letter boxes are emptied, the letters, etc., are seized upon by eager hands for the purpose of being faced, that is, put into order right way up to receive the impression of the date stamp, which cancels the postage stamps affixed. At the same time those letters on which insufficient postage has been paid are detected and thrown out to be surcharged. Having been properly faced, the letters are passed on for the purpose of being stamped, which is an important operation, for not only does the impression cancel the postage stamp and indicate both the office the letter has passed through and the time of collection, but it also affords a clue in case of inquiry to the person through whose hands it has passed, because each stamper has to sign a book underneath an impression of the stamp used by him. The stamper also keeps a tally of the letters passing through his hands by making an impression of his date stamp on a separate piece of paper after every fiftieth letter stamped, and in this manner the number of letters dealt with at the General Post Office is ascertained, which at the present time is roughly half-a-million a night. As may be imagined, the letters pass through the stampers' hands with lightning rapidity.

From the stampers the letters pass to the sorters, to whom they are taken in bundles by carrier-boys directly they are stamped. The sorting is divided into three stages, the first stage being into divisions of the principal railway lines, together with some of the more important towns, such as Liverpool, Manchester, etc. The second stage consists in sorting the letters into lines of railway, and the third into roads, that is to say, under the head of the large towns on each line. In the case of letters destined for places served by the Travelling Post Office, the letters are sorted only into the lines of railways on which they have to be conveyed, the remainder of the sorting process being performed, as we have seen, on the journey. With the sortation of the letters into towns they are ready for tying-up and bagging, preparatory to their being taken to the mail-carts, which convey them to the various railway termini. The various sorting tables are fitted with pigeon-holes, which are

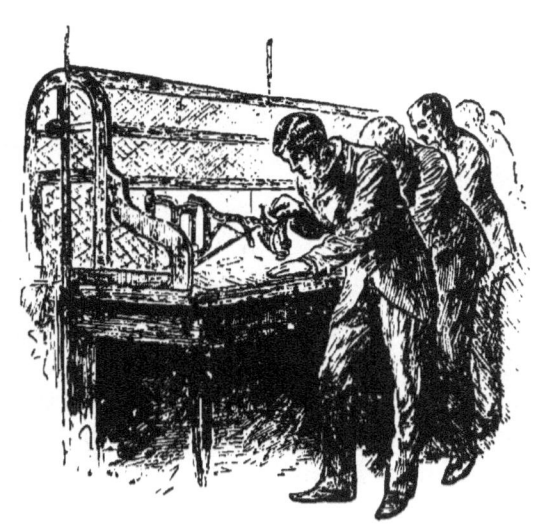

STAMPING.

divided according to the requirements of the sortation performed at each table ; and in the case of the tables where the primary sortation takes place there is added to the pigeon-holes a compartment labelled " Blind," which is intended for the reception of those letters the addresses on which are not decipherable to the ordinary sorter. For the sorting of those letters which are in the nature of packets, baskets take the place of the ordinary pigeon-holes.

Leaving the sorting hall and going upstairs, the visitor reaches by a tortuous route the *Newspaper Room*, where facing, stamping, and sorting on a bulkier scale is to be witnessed. An interesting feature of the duties here is the periodical seizure of bundles of the newspapers and packets for the purpose of opening them to see whether the regulation that no written communication should be enclosed has not been contravened. That many attempts are made to evade the regulation is undoubted, and the officials well know how necessary it is to keep a sharp look-out in this direction. The following is an amusing method of evasion frequently attempted, and not without success. It may be known that the *Queen* newspaper often issues cut patterns of dresses or other feminine garments, which, if sent with the paper through the post, entails extra postage over and above the ordinary newspaper rate. To avoid this, the sender of the paper will, if artfully disposed, and if, as is often the case, he is sending another weekly paper, say the *Graphic*, to the same address, take the cut pattern out of the *Queen* and place it in the *Graphic*, because the officials, while always on the alert as regards the former paper, naturally pass the latter by without suspicion. Of the morality of the proceeding it is unnecessary to speak, but to the officials concerned it might be whispered *verb. sap.*

The *Foreign Room* is specially interesting because the letters are, as the visitor knows, presently to be scudding on their way to every habitable quarter of the globe. In the *Registered Letter Branch* the system of sorting is somewhat encumbered, owing to the principle on which the registered letter system is carried out, requiring everyone through whose hands

each letter passes to give a receipt for it.   To overcome the difficulty, which the working out in detail of
this principle in dealing with so many letters as are
nightly handled at the General Post Office would
involve, forms of receipt are made to take the place
of the letters themselves, with the result that only the
clerk who opens the in-coming bag and the clerk who
makes up the
out-going bag
really handle
the   letters.
Small   blue
bags are pro-
vided for pack-
ing the regis-
tered letters by
themselves,
these bags be-
ing put subse-
quently in the
general de-
spatch bags.

THE HOSPITAL.

The *Hospital*
and the *Blind-
Room* are to
the   visitor
features that never fail to interest.   To the former
are carried all the letters and packets which have
been posted, and have become in such a bad condition
that the contents are in danger of getting astray in
transmission.   It is hardly credible how careless
many of the public are in regard to the posting of
their correspondence, but of this there can be no
doubt when we notice the hundreds of letters that

have been posted quite open, bearing not the slightest evidence of any effort having been made to fasten them. Such letters, together with the fragile articles badly or insecurely packed, form a source of much extra trouble to the Post Office, inasmuch as the work left undone by a thoughtless public has to be completed by the members of the postal hospital.

To the *Blind-Room* are brought all the letters which bear insufficient, misspelt, or illegible addresses, and which the sorters have thrown into the pigeon-hole labelled "Blind." Here the clerks, selected from amongst the most experienced and skilled sorting clerks, have to decipher writing which others have given up as a hopeless task. Truly, one comes across some of the most curious and eccentric specimens both of caligraphy and orthography in the "blind" office, and the fact that so many of these badly written and ill-spelt missives are sent on their way through the skill of the "blind" officers, as is the case, is strong testimony to their high intelligence. The difficulties these officers have to contend with may be fairly appreciated when it is known that such addresses as " Haselfeach in no famtshere " interpreted as, " Hazelbeach, Northamptonshire," or, " Santlings Hilewite," interpreted as, " St. Helen's, Isle of Wight," or again, " Coneyach lamentick a siliam," interpreted as, " Colney Hatch Lunatic Asylum," were all promptly deciphered and sent on their way. There are some towns which give no end of trouble both to the writer and the officials, as witness, Ashby-de-la-Zouch, which is spelt in fifty different ways. " Has bedellar-such " would appear to be the general spelling among the poorer classes. The following is a veritable copy of an address for the town referred to :

"Ash Bedles in such
for John Horsel, grinder
in the county of Lestyshire."

A little time ago a letter was posted to the "25th of March, London," which through the ready wit of one of the "blind" officers was correctly delivered to the wife of the judge of that name. Even more

DECIPHERING THE "BLIND" LETTERS.

puzzling was the letter addressed by a trustful correspondent at Ludlow to "the gentleman who looked at a house near Cleobury Mortimer a little time ago, Bilston," and left it to the Post Office to discover this particular individual in a town of 25,000 inhabitants. Within four days of posting, it was duly delivered to the gentleman for whom it was intended. But there

are cases which baffle even the keen-witted officials
of the *Blind-Room*. It was, for example, only when
opened in the Returned Letter Office that the missive
addressed to " Mister Willy wot brinds de Baber in
Lang Gaster were te gal is" was discovered to be
intended for the editor of a Lancaster paper "where
the gaol is." " Uncle John, Hopposite the Church,
London, Hingland," is an address that proved to be
too vague even for the " *Blind-Room*," aided as it is
with the most complete dictionaries, directories, and
gazetteers ; while a letter addressed, " Ann M——
Oiley White, Amshire," was, in the absence of the
name of any town, undeliverable, although no doubt
existed that it was destined for the Isle of Wight,
Hampshire. A valuable collection of the most
curious addresses on letters is kept in the *Blind-
Room*, where visitors are permitted to dip into the
pages of this most interesting volume.

As the clock hand nears the hour of eight, the rush
of work is coming to an end, and the point of interest
is to be found at the north end of the great hall,
where mail-bags are being rapidly filled, tied, labelled,
and sealed. In the yard outside is waiting a long
row of mail-carts, into which porters shoot the bags
with the rapidity and precision born of constant
practice. Each cart is labelled with the name of the
line it is going to, and a clerk stands by to tick-off
the number of bags deposited. Under the lurid glare
of the electric light a busy scene is enacted in the
yard by a throng of active workers, and it is not
until a quarter past eight that the lid of the last cart
is slammed down, and the mails of the evening finally
despatched. The carts rattle along the streets at the
highest speed to the great railway termini, where the

bags are speedily transferred to the mail vans attached to each of the out-going trains. So end the labours of the day in the Circulation Office, so far as the night mails are concerned, at St. Martin's le Grand.

AT THE FOOT OF THE SHOOT AT EIGHT P.M.

It may be fitting to conclude this chapter with a word as to the work of delivering the mails. Arrived at the towns for which they are destined, the bags are quickly transferred from the train to the station, whence they are at once taken by mail-cart or hand-. barrow to the Post Office, where they are seized, their "throats cut," and their contents poured on the sorting tables. Once again they pass through the ordeal of being stamped, after which the sorting clerks take them over and arrange them in the different boxes. Some of the clerks prepare the letters for the post-men, while others do so for the subordinate Post Offices and rural messengers, these letters being despatched thence either by train, mail-cart, or rural messenger. The town postmen, having received their bundles of letters, retire to their own room, where they arrange the letters in convenient order for house-to-house delivery. The newspapers, it should perhaps be stated, are handed over direct to the postmen for sortation without being stamped.

In some of the large centres, as for example at Edinburgh, the postmen are taken out in vans known as accelerators, and each man, as the van reaches the beginning of his "walk," drops therefrom and com-mences his delivery. Although every possible means are adopted by the Post Office to effect delivery of the correspondence posted, yet from various causes there always remain some which are undeliverable. Standing alone, the number of such letters makes a respectable show, being over seventeen millions in the year, but taken in relation to the total number of letters, etc., posted in the year—namely, over 3000 millions, the proportion is very insignificant. The unde-livered letters find their way to the various returned letter offices, where they are dealt with as circum-stances may permit. A large number are re-issued to corrected addresses, about half are returned to the senders, while the rest remain undisposable.

CHAPTER VI.

ABOUT POSTAGE STAMPS.

AN inalienable factor in the postal system, not only of this country, but also of every other country throughout the world, is that humble little adhesive label generally known as the postage stamp, for it has proved the only satisfactory method of prepaying postage. It would be. of considerable interest could we discover who was the inventor of these useful and universally popular little tokens of " postage paid " ; but the matter is one, as it will probably remain, of great uncertainty. From one source we learn that they originated in 1653 with a M. de Velayer, who established, under royal authority, a private post in Paris, placing boys at the corners of the streets for the reception of letters, which were to be' wrapped up in certain *envelopes.* These envelopes, some of which are said to be still in existence, had no device or design upon them, but simply a few printed instructions. Shopkeepers in the immediate neighbourhood sold the envelopes at the price of one sou. The envelopes, or tickets, were attached to the letters, or wrapped round them in such a manner that the postmen could remove and retain them on delivering the letters.

It would be difficult to determine whether or not

this practice gave rise subsequently to the idea of postage stamps in our own country, but it seems somewhat improbable that there is any such connection, seeing that the first proposals in England for the payment of postage in this manner were not made until 1836. The first we hear of the idea of using such stamps is in the discussions which took place relative to the proposal to reduce the newspaper postage from fourpence to a penny, when Mr. Matthew D. Hill, the member for Hull, referred to a proposal that Mr. Charles Knight had made suggesting the collection of the new postage for newspapers by means of stamped wrappers sold at a penny each. According to the Report of the Select Committee on Postage in 1837–38, a somewhat similar proposal was made by Mr. Charles Whiting, with the view of defeating the then too common system of evasion in the manner of addressing newspapers where all kinds of changes were rung in the words constituting the address. This proposal was, however, never taken up.

The prepayment of postage was, as has been seen, one of Rowland Hill's proposals, and for this reason it is commonly supposed that he was also the originator of the postage stamp, but this is not the fact ; nor did Rowland Hill ever lay claim to the suggestion, which, however, he carefully elaborated and perfected, and made use of in connection with his own scheme. His first intention was that the postage should be prepaid by the payment of the money over the counter, but he subsequently came to the conclusion that the purposes of the public and the Post Office would be better served by the use of some kind of stamp, or stamped covers, for letters. This arrangement he brought forward before the Commissioners of Post Office Inquiry in 1837, to whom he fully explained it, referring to it as Mr. Knight's "excellent suggestion." The following extract from the Commissioners' Ninth Report, giving as it does a brief description of the proposed arrangement, will be read at this distant period with much interest :—

(1.) That stamped covers, or sheets of paper, or small vignette stamps — the latter if used to be gummed on the face of the letter—to be supplied to the public from the Stamp Office, and sold at such a price as to include the postage. Letters so stamped to be treated in all respects as franks.

(2.) That as covers of various prices would be required for packets of various weights, each should have the weight it is entitled to carry legibly printed upon the stamp.

(3.) That the stamp of the receiving-house should be stuck upon the superscription or duty stamp to prevent the letter being used a second time.

(4.) The vignette stamps being portable, persons could carry them in their pocket-books.

Such were the main features of the new arrangement for prepaying letters which were laid before the Commissioners of Post Office Inquiry, who, as well as the Committee on Postage in 1837–38, carefully considered the matter, and finally arrived at a favourable conclusion ; in consequence of which a clause providing for the use of such stamps and stamped covers was included in the subsequent Penny Postage Act.

Some difficulty was found in choosing between the use of simple adhesive labels, or stamped paper, and the use of stamped envelopes, and considerable difference of opinion appears to have existed on the point. The first suggestion was to use stamped paper representing different charges, and which, when folded in a particular manner, would expose the stamp to view and frank the letter. In those days much importance was attached to the letter and the address being on the same sheet of paper, which, indeed, was a point of legal moment, and hence this proposal to use stamped paper found numerous advocates amongst the members of the legal and mercantile communities. On the other hand, separate stamped envelopes were represented by their supporters as being far more convenient, and this idea seems to have been the more popular one.

The Government decided to adopt both ideas, and a proclamation was issued on the 23rd of August, 1839, inviting "all artists, men of science, and the public in general to offer proposals as to the manner in which the stamp may best be brought into use." Foreign governments were apprised of the matter by the Foreign Secretary, and suggestions were invited from all parts of the world. The Treasury offered two prizes of £200 and £100 respectively for the proposals which they might deem "most deserving of attention," and the offer was sufficiently attractive to bring in nearly 3000 proposals.

As regards envelopes, the design sent in by the late Mr. Mulready, R.A., was, as is well known, selected, but its career was a short-lived one. Engraved in wood, the design of the envelopes was intended to celebrate allegorically the triumph of the post by means of a host of emblematical figures, and they were printed in black ink for the penny postage, and in blue for the twopenny postage. They met, however, with such small favour that they were withdrawn from use six months after their first issue.

The postage stamp, for which over a thousand designs were sent, proved a lasting success. The chief conditions were that it should be simple, handy, and easily placed upon paper, and also of such a nature as to make forgery difficult, if not impossible. Messrs. Bacon & Petch were the designers of the original stamp, which was engraved on a steel die by Mr. Charles Heath. The portrait of the Queen

POSTAGE ONE PENNY.

THE MULREADY ENVELOPE.

is stated to have been taken from a drawing by Mr. Henry Corbould from Wyon's city medal. First printed in black, the colour was two years subsequently changed to brown, with a view to perfect the process of obliteration and the more easily to detect the dishonest use of old stamps; and again, some time afterwards, it was altered to the long-familiar red colour for the same reason.

Postage stamps were first brought into use in May, 1840, five months after the introduction of Penny

Postage, and speedily became an assured success. Issued at first only for the value of one penny, they were gradually extended to other values as their use became generally adopted. Of course there was not wanting the usual amount of opposition to a scheme of so innovating a character, and it was considered by many that the plan would prove "inconvenient and foreign to the habits of Englishmen." It is, indeed, hard to credit the various objections which were raised against the adoption of the proposed stamps, many being of quite a ridiculous character. Thus, the Post Office Secretary argued that "half-ounce letters weighing an ounce or above" were one out of nine classes of letters to which the proposed stamp could not be applied, but Rowland Hill naïvely observed in reply that "letters exhibiting so remarkable a peculiarity might present difficulties with which he was not prepared to deal." The most conclusive answer to all arguments and objections was, however, the wonderful popularity postage stamps at once acquired, some idea of which may be gained from the fact that, in the first fifteen years after they were brought into use, three thousand million stamps were manufactured in order to meet public requirements. Various changes in form, design, and colour have, of course, been made from time to time, and postage stamps now range in value from one halfpenny to five pounds.

One of the most important improvements made in connection with their use was that of perforation. For many years the stamps could only be separated from each other in the sheet by the primitive process of cutting with scissors or knives. In 1847, a Mr. Archer proposed to the then Postmaster-General a machine which he thought might be made " to pierce the sheet of stamps with holes, so that each sheet might be torn apart." The proposal was favoured by the Post Office, and Mr. Archer's machine, which he had patented, was purchased for £4000. It was not, however, very useful in practice, and had to be considerably improved upon by the stamp authorities before it was made to answer public wants.

The work of manufacturing postage stamps is carried on for the Government by a firm of contractors who, after completing the various processes through which they have to pass, deliver the stamps into the custody of the Inland Revenue Department. This department undertakes the work of distributing the stamps to the various Post Offices throughout the United Kingdom, the quantities sent out daily being enormous. The value of the stamps kept in stock at Somerset House is said to be also enormous, the stamps being stored in large safes distributed over the various rooms in the basement of the Inland Revenue Office, and at such distances as to minimise the risk of entire destruction by fire.

The undoubted value of stamps for the collection of postage soon led, as may be imagined, to their being utilised for Inland Revenue collection, in which capacity they have now long served. For many years a distinctive stamp was used, commonly known as the "receipt stamp," but for the past seventeen years or more the ordinary postage has fulfilled the combined purpose of collecting postage and Inland Revenue. The benefits which accrued to the public from this change can hardly be over-estimated, for whereas a postage stamp is everywhere to be had, it was not in the old days always so easy a matter to obtain the distinctive Inland Revenue stamp.

Another most useful office which the postage stamp fulfils is the prepayment of telegrams. When, in 1870, the Government took over the telegraphs of the country, the collection of the revenue from this source was naturally made by means of the well-tried postage stamps, but in 1876 it was considered desirable to introduce a new and distinctive set of stamps to be used purely for telegraphic purposes. In 1880, however, the principle of the unified stamp had been brought into operation and found to answer very satisfactorily, and it was soon after applied to telegrams, and the old practice was thus reverted to.

The use of postage stamps in connection with Postal Orders and Savings Bank Deposits has become well known. In the former case they aid most usefully in remitting small sums by making up odd amounts not provided for in the fixed amounts of Postal Orders, and are also useful in paying the extra commission which becomes due on lapsed orders. The privilege of being able to remit odd amounts by stamps has greatly enhanced the popularity of Postal Orders, and many thousand pounds worth of stamps are annually used in this manner. Many years ago, not long, indeed, after stamps were brought into general use, the convenience of remitting small sums of money by means of postage stamps was speedily perceived by the public, and taken advantage of. When, however, the Money Order rates, and registered letter fees were reduced, the necessity for so using them diminished, and with the existing cheap and ready system of Postal Orders it was almost entirely removed. The practice, indeed, is one that the Post Office authorities has always rather discouraged than approved of, as it is considered to offer temptations to letter-stealing. In regard to Post Office Savings Bank Deposits, postage stamps are of manifest advantage, as it enables those who cannot afford to save a shilling at a time (the minimum limit of deposit at one time), to save penny by penny by using one of the printed forms provided for the purpose, and obtainable at any Post Office. This scheme was first tried in 1880, and there can be no doubt that, from the extensive use which is made of the system, it has proved a great benefit to a numerous class, and has engendered and fostered thrift in many quarters where otherwise the pence would probably have found their way into less advantageous channels.

A fair idea of the general use of postage stamps may be gathered from the fact that the number of letters posted in the year in this country is at the rate of three thousand millions, while the number of telegrams delivered is at the rate of seventy-nine millions in the year. These astounding figures require no comment, and, as can be imagined, the number of postage stamps which they represent must be something fabulous. Associate letters and correspondence generally, as we are bound to do, with education, literature, science, and commerce, and it must be owned that the foregoing statistics proclaim, with no uncertain sound, the advance which has been made within the past sixty years in civilisation in this country.

Not the least interesting feature in connection with postage stamps is the mania of the stamp collector. Of course, as we know, that mania forms an epoch in the life of every schoolboy, but it is surprising to learn how widely the craze exists, or has existed, among

the older members of the community. Philatelic
societies, indeed, now exist, the *raison d'être* of which
is the collection and examination of postage stamps
of all countries. Although the mania runs high
nowadays, it does not appear to be at such a height
as that which it had reached about the year 1862,
when, according to the late Mr. Lewins, crowds
nightly congregated in Birchin Lane, to the exceeding
annoyance and wonder of the uninitiated, "where
ladies and gentlemen of all ages and ranks, from
Cabinet ministers to crossing sweepers, were busy,
with album and portfolio in hand, buying, selling, or
exchanging," which scenes are now known to have
been the beginnings of what may almost be termed a
new trade. Very high prices are now asked and
received for some of the rarer kinds of stamps, and it
is remarkable what enormous sums an enthusiast will
pay for a genuine specimen of a very rare stamp.

CHAPTER VII.

OCEAN POSTAGE.

THE Packet Service forms one of the most important adjuncts of the Post Office, and, at a very early date, ships were employed for the conveyance of letters, etc., abroad. Even in the early days of the Post Office, the packet service was regarded as one of supreme importance, for we have it on the highest authority that, when the office of Postmaster-General was held jointly by two Ministers of the Crown, one took charge principally of the inland business, while the other managed the packets. At that time, we are told, the service was undeveloped, and contracts for the work had just begun to be thought of, so that the Post Office authorities had to build packets as well as to furnish and man them, and when the ships were unfit for work they had to be disposed of.

In times of war, too, these ships had to be armed, for they were required to fight when occasion arose, so that they were armed as war-vessels. The packet service in those days had many difficulties to contend with. Of course the vessels were very much at the mercy of the elements; the men on board, on account of their semi-official character, were more than ordinarily difficult of control; and the French and other privateers, with which the seas then abounded, gave much trouble to the packets.

The Postmasters-General were also required to see, as we learn, that the vessels were despatched with sufficient stores and men, and so, during the continuance of strife, their duties never flagged, and their energies were continually on the stretch. The official records in existence show that this picture is not overdrawn, while it is amply confirmed by some of the letters from the Postmasters-General to their agents. In one, for example, they say, "We are very uneasy, and shall be till we hear the stores are safely arrived with you, which we impatiently wish." In another, they are "concerned to find the letters brought by your boat (from the West Indies) to be so *consumed by the ratts*, that we cannot find out to whom they belong." In yet another, they tell one of their captains that his "letter of the 4th was very welcome after our many apprehensions of some misfortune having happened to the expedition." The following letter to their agent at Harwich partakes of a disciplinary nature:— "Mr. Edisbury, The woman whose complaint we herewith send you, having given us much trouble upon the same, we desire you will enquire into the same and see justice done her, believing she may have had her brandy stole from her by the sailors, We are, your affectionate friends,—R. C. T. F." The Postmasters-General evidently knew their men, and as the good spirit was no doubt lost beyond recovery, let us hope the poor woman received due compensation.

Mr. Scudamore, to whom we are indebted for rescuing these records of past Post Office history from oblivion, also remarks that "what with scolding an agent once because 'he had not provided a suffici-

ency of pork and beef for the Prince;' again, because
'he had bought powder at Falmouth that would have
been cheaper in London;' again, because 'he had
stirred up a mutiny between a captain and his men,
which was unhandsome conduct in him;' again,
because 'he has not ordered the *Dolphin* to sail,
though the wind is marked westerly in the wind
journals;' what with bringing Captain Clies to trial
'for that he had spoken words reflecting on the
Royal Family, which the Postmasters-General took
particular unkind of him;' and reprimanding another
for 'breaking open the portmanteau of Mons. Raoul
(a gentleman passenger), and spoiling him of a parcel
of snuff;' what with purchasing new vessels, stores,
and provisions, and ordering the old ones to be sold
by inch of candle—with all these cases, one sees that
our Postmasters-General had enough to do."

Many of these letters are dated in the middle of
the night, and at other extraordinary hours: all are
remarkable for clearness, compactness, and precision;
and in some, as, for instance, in one very long letter
dismissing a contumacious agent, "we see," adds
Mr. Scudamore, "that the writers were worthy con-
temporaries of that most English of all English
writers, Daniel Defoe." It seems to have been essential that all the letters and mandates should be
signed by both the Postmasters-General—Sir Robert
Cotton and Sir Thomas Frankland—for there are
frequent notices in the records to the effect that
"your business cannot be attended to until Sir
Thomas Frankland, who hath a fitte of gout, shall
be somewhat recovered."

The packets in those days, when war raged for
so many years, gave the Postmasters-General the

greatest anxiety. Their orders to the captains of such vessels are urgent, that they shall run while they can, fight when they can no longer run, and throw the mails overboard when fighting will no longer avail. The state of the mail service to Ireland at this time is well illustrated by the fact that in 1693 a piteous petition was received from James Vickers, the captain of the *Grace Dogger*, who, while his vessel lay in Dublin Bay waiting until the tide would take him over the bar, was seized by a French privateer, the captain of which stripped the *Grace Dogger* of her rigging, sails, spars, and yards, and of all the furniture "wherewith she had been provided for the due accommodation of passengers, leaving not so much as a spoone, or a nail hooke to hang anything on." The vessel was finally ransomed to James Vickers for fifty guineas, which sum, with the cost of other losses, the Postmasters-General had to pay. The result of this and similar misfortunes was that the Postmasters-General resolved to build swift packet-boats that should escape the enemy, but built them so low in the water that a report states "we doe find that in blowy weather they take in soe much water that the men are constantly wet all through, and can noe ways goe below to change themselves, being obliged to keep the hatches shut to save the vessels from sinking, which is such a discouragement to the sailors that it will be of the greatest difficulty to get any to endure such hardshippes in the winter weather." It is difficult to realise this state of things now, when the mail packet service is performed by splendid steam vessels of extraordinary power and speed—the voyage from Dover to Calais being performed in little over an hour, and that from

Holyhead to Kingstown in two hours and three-quarters; while the mails for the United States, India, and the Colonies are conveyed with the utmost rapidity and regularity by magnificent fleets of the finest steam vessels in the world. The mail packet service is now, indeed, one of the most expensive, as well as important, branches of the postal service. In the seventeenth and eighteenth centuries it was under the control of the Post Office authorities; it then passed under the authority of the Admiralty until 1860, when it again came into the hands of the Post Office.

In 1853 a Treasury Committee was appointed to inquire into the contract packet service, and they reported that "it is unreasonable to expect that any person or association of persons should incur the expense and risk of building vessels, forming costly establishments, and opening a new line of communication at a heavy outlay of capital without some security that they would be allowed to continue the service long enough to reap some benefits from their undertaking. It must be borne in mind that the expensive vessels built for the conveyance of the mails, at a high rate of speed, are not in demand for the purposes of ordinary traffic, and cannot therefore be withdrawn and applied to another service at a short notice. . . . The value of the services thus rendered to the State cannot, we think, be measured by a mere reference to the amount of the postal revenue, or even of the commercial advantages accruing from it. It is undoubtedly startling at first sight to see that the immediate pecuniary result of the packet system is a loss to the revenue of about £325,000 a-year; but, although this circumstance

shows the necessity for a careful revision of the
service, and though we believe that much may be
done to make the service self-supporting, we do not
consider that the money thus expended is to be
regarded, even from a fiscal point of view, as a
national loss."

The British Post Office first adopted the conveyance of mails in steamers in 1821. The Holyhead
Station for Ireland, and Dover for the Continent, were
selected for the first experiments. After fruitless
negotiations with steam packet companies, it was
determined to build vessels at the cost of the
Government. Eventually six such vessels were
stationed at Holyhead, and several others at Dover
and elsewhere. The report of the Commissioners of
Revenue Inquiry led to the gradual introduction of
commercial contracts for this service, the first of
which was made by the Postmaster-General in 1833
with the Mona Isle Steam Packet Company, to run
steamers twice a-week between Liverpool and
Douglas. In the following year the General Steam
Navigation Company contracted to carry the mails
twice a-week between London and Rotterdam and
London and Hamburg for £17,000 a-year. This
contract remained in force until 1853, when these mails
were transferred to the Ostend route. In 1837 a
contract was made with Mr. Richard Bourne to
convey the mail weekly from Falmouth to Vigo,
Oporto, Lisbon, and Gibraltar for £29,600 a-year.
In 1843 it was transferred to the Peninsular and
Oriental Company, the port of Southampton was
substituted for Falmouth, and the trips limited to
three monthly, the subsidy being proportionately
reduced. 1839 was marked by the establishment of

a fortnightly mail between Liverpool, Halifax, and Boston by contract between the Postmaster-General and Samuel Cunard of Halifax, at £60,000 a-year. Soon the port was made alternately Boston and New York; and with this change the contract had greater activity, weekly trips being required instead of fortnightly, and the subsidy being raised by the renewal

THE S.S. "WILLIAM FAWCETT."
*The first P. and O. Steamship employed in carrying Mails. Tonnage, 206;
Horse-power, 60.*

contract of 1850 to £173,340 a-year, with certain contingent allowances in addition.

In subsequent years contracts were made with the great steamship companies for the conveyance of the mails to the most distant parts of the world, into which it would be tedious to enter in detail.

Since those days the mail services have been per-

G

fected in almost all respects, and when the Pilgrim
Fathers settled in America 'they could never have
imagined that the mails would traverse the Atlantic
in less than six days in floating palaces like the
Teutonic ; nor could the East India Company have
anticipated that the mails which occupied six months
in voyaging round the Cape in a sailing vessel would
complete the journey in seventeen days by means of
the splendid steam vessels of the Peninsular and
Oriental Company ; while it would have been equally
incredible to the first settlers in Australia that the
vast distance intervening between them and the
mother country would be accomplished in thirty-two
days.

The great facilities which thus exist for communication with India and the colonies have, of course, been
still further enhanced by the reduction of the postage
to 2½d. for a letter under half-an-ounce in weight.

The feat of delivering letters in London within a
week of their despatch from New York was accomplished for the first time in October, 1889, and the
following is the record of the first trip. The Inman
steamer, *City of New York,* and the White Star liner,
Teutonic, passed Sandy Hook at 7.35 A.M. and
7.51 A.M. respectively, on Wednesday the 15th of
October. Mails were carried by both vessels, those
on board the *City of New York* numbering 302 sacks,
and those on the *Teutonic* 31 sacks. The bulk of the
mails was sent by the Inman steamer, while only
correspondence specially addressed was forwarded by
the *Teutonic.* The White Star liner, however, made
the quicker passage, and arrived off Roches Point at
12.45 P.M. on the 21st, or 1 hour 47 minutes sooner
than her rival. The mails were sent on from

Queenstown by the 1.40 P.M. mail train, and reached London with the Irish mail at 6.50 A.M. on Wednesday the 22nd, in time for the correspondence to be distributed by the second delivery in the city and other town districts of London, and for the closed mails for the Continent to be forwarded by the first day mails. The mails conveyed by the *City of New York* were landed at Queenstown at 2.30 P.M., and every effort was made to overtake the *Teutonic's* mail by the employment of a special train to Dublin, a special boat to Holyhead, and a special train thence to London. By these means the mail reached London only 2 hours 18 minutes after that conveyed by the *Teutonic*, and the letters, etc., fell into the next or third delivery throughout London, and the Continental mails were forwarded by the second day mails at about 10.30 A.M. If this mail had been forwarded from Queenstown by the ordinary arrangements it would not have reached London until late in the day on Wednesday, and consequently letters, etc., would not have been in the hands of the public before four or five o'clock.

It only remains to add, in concluding this chapter, that the Overland Route by which the mails are conveyed to India by the direct route, through the Mediterranean and over the Isthmus of Suez, was the result of the indefatigable exertions of the late Lieutenant Waghorn, that route being first used in the year 1835.

It may also be stated that nearly a million pounds are paid annually for mail packet contracts.

CHAPTER VIII.

TELEGRAPHS AND TELEPHONES.

THAT inter-communication by telegraphy should become a collateral service with that of the post seems to us in the present day only natural, and it was in the fitness of things human that sooner or later the Government should take over the electric wires of the country, and place them under the control of the Post Office authorities. The actual transfer of the various telegraphic systems existing throughout the country took place on the 5th of February, 1870, although the financial agreements between the Government and the Telegraph Companies took effect from the 29th of January of that year ; but, like most kindred reforms that have been effected in this country, public agitation for the change had existed for very many years prior to the realisation of the desired object.

The first perhaps to broach the subject publicly was Mr. Thomas Allan, a well-known engineer, who so far back as the year 1854, issued a paper, entitled "Reasons for the Government annexing an electric telegraph system to the General Post Office," in which he urged uniformity of charges, and an extended area of working, as the chief advantages of his proposal. He was followed by many others, who from time to time published schemes for the establishment of a postal telegraphic system; but the more formal and vigorous agitation in favour of the transfer of the telegraphs to the Post Office was not commenced until 1865, when the matter was taken up by the Edinburgh Chambers of Commerce, and in the following year by the Associated Chambers of Commerce, who forwarded a petition embodying the proposition to both Houses of Parliament. The theme, indeed, presently became one for general discussion, and there was no uncertain note as to the direction towards which the arguments tended, for public opinion manifested itself strongly in favour of the transfer, so strongly, in fact, that it may be almost said that, as the Duke of Montrose, who was then Postmaster-General, put it, the Post Office was invited to adopt the measure by the Chambers of Commerce throughout the United Kingdom, and by almost the entire press of the country.

If the conditions under which the telegraphic arrangements of the country were at that time carried out be remembered, it is not surprising that public feeling should have been so strongly in favour of the change. In the first place, the rates were high and wholly devoid of uniformity, as may be judged by the tariff which the principal telegraph companies had agreed to under the provisions of the Telegraph Act of 1863. Under that tariff the charge in Great Britain was one shilling for a twenty-word message over distances not exceeding 100 miles; 1s. 6d. over distances exceeding 100 and not exceeding 200 miles; and 2s. if exceeding the latter mentioned distance, half-rates over and above the original rate being charged for additions of ten words or less. For telegrams between Great Britain and Ireland the charge ranged from 3s. to 6s.

But that was not all, for the foregoing tariff was limited in its operations to certain lines and districts, beyond which many unfavourable exceptions arose. Thus, there were as many as twenty-five branch lines of telegraphs belonging to companies other than those that had agreed to the above-mentioned tariff, and on which lines there were about 475 stations. For messages transmitted over those branch lines extra charges were made over and above the ordinary tariff, which were always high and sometimes exorbitant in proportion to the ordinary tariff. For example, a telegram of twenty words from London to Granton, which is three miles from Edinburgh, was made up of 2s. the charge to Edinburgh, and 1s. the additional charge to Granton. Again, the charge for a twenty words' telegram from London to Bournemouth, which is seven miles from Poole, was made up of 1s. the charge to Poole, and 2s. the extra charge to Bournemouth. Moreover, there were stations in connection with one of the companies where an extra fee of 6d. was charged for forwarding or receiving messages as a fee to the station master for his trouble.

A varying tariff such as that indicated, framed primarily upon distances, and secondarily upon routes, was obviously difficult for popular comprehension, and there can be no doubt that the complexity of the charges gave rise to so much uncertainty as to what would have to be paid for a telegram that many persons were prevented from using the wires who would otherwise have freely done so.

Another disadvantage keenly felt under the system of the old telegraph companies was the very insufficient provision made for small towns and the suburbs of large towns, and the almost entire dependence of rural districts upon railway stations, at many of which the service was only occasional, and at but few of which was there a regular messenger. In many cases, too, the telegraphic lines of the railway and telegraph companies were identical, a circumstance which resulted in the further disadvantage to the public of the railway messages being always accorded priority, thus leading to much inconvenience and many vexatious delays.

Enough has probably been said to indicate that there was very good ground for the agitation that ultimately led to the transfer. The community was not unnaturally growing weary of a system under which the various companies acted practically in combination, and virtually exercised a monopoly, charging almost what they liked, and acting more or less high-handedly in their administration. It was therefore hailed as a step in the right direction when Lord Stanley of Alderley, as Postmaster-General, instructed Mr. Frank Ives Scudamore, one of the Post Office Secretaries, to thoroughly inquire into and report upon the whole subject. A change of Government in 1866 prevented Lord Stanley of Alderley from giving consideration to Mr. Scudamore's exhaustive report, which, however, was duly presented to Parliament, and the matter hung fire until two years later, when in February, 1868, the subject was revived by the Duke of Montrose, who was then at the head of the Post Office. There was, of course, considerable opposition on the part of the Telegraph

Companies to the proposed transfer, but seeing that not only the public generally, but also the Government, were in favour of such a change, that opposition was overcome without much difficulty. A Bill authorising the purchase of the telegraphs of the country was brought into Parliament in 1868, and after being subjected to the searching scrutiny of a Parliamentary Committee, became law before the end of that session. Before, however, the Act could come into operation it was necessary that a money bill should be passed, which was done the following session, and on the 5th of February, 1870, the telegraphic systems of the United Kingdom were completely and successfully transferred to the Post Office.

The results of that important event have, as we know, proved in all respects, and to all sections of the community, of the most beneficial character. In the first place, the transfer swept away the complex and exorbitant charges which prevailed under the companies' systems, substituting a simplified, reduced, and uniform tariff for the transmission of telegrams throughout the United Kingdom. It will be remembered that at first the Post Office charge was uniformly one shilling for twenty words, with three-pence extra for every additional five words or fraction thereof, the names and addresses of both senders and addressees not being included. This tariff was not, however, decided upon without considerable discussion when the Telegraph Bill was before the House of Commons, the adoption of a sixpenny rate being strongly advocated. Mr. Scudamore himself was at one time in favour of such a rate, but, after looking closely into the matter, he wisely determined that the time was not ripe for so low a tariff, and it was not until fifteen years later, namely, in 1885, that the present sixpenny rate was introduced.

Another distinct advantage derived by the public from the transfer was the extension of the wires lying outside town populations to Post Offices in the centre of such populations, the extension of the wires already carried into large cities towards the suburbs, and the extension of the wires from towns into rural and other districts unprovided with telegraphic accommodation. The combined effect of these extensions has, of course, been to bring the telegraphs closer to the population generally, and to save time and the cost of porterage to the senders and receivers of telegrams. Then, again, the transfer has effected a complete separation of commercial telegraph wires from those of railway companies, with the result of removing those inconveniences and vexatious delays of which the telegraphing public had good cause to complain in the days of the old companies.

But the most important result, after the uniform rate, is perhaps in connection with the newspaper press, for the transfer created free trade in the collection of news for the press, with low rates for the transmission of such news, no matter by what or by how many agencies it may be collected. Prior to the transfer the Telegraph Companies were in combination for the collection and transmission of news, and although their rates were not very high, yet as they had the command of telegraphic communication in the United Kingdom, the newspaper proprietors who required telegraph news were compelled to resort to them for it, and to take what they were willing to supply ; and this monopoly without doubt tended to check the distribution of news throughout the country. The Telegraph Act of 1868 provided a tariff of 1s. per 100 words from 6 P.M. to 9 A.M., and 1s. for 75 words from 9 A.M. to 6 P.M. for news messages to a single address, with an additional charge of 2d. for every additional address to which such message may be sent. No undue priority was to be given in respect of such rates to any newspaper proprietor or publisher. This tariff, which has ever since been in operation, has undoubtedly worked well, and the effect it has had in increasing the speed of telegraphic news throughout the country could not be better evidenced than by the columns of our leading news-papers. And especially is this influence now felt in connection with political meetings, events of import-ance, or race-meetings.

Nearly thirty years have passed since the assump-tion of the control of the Telegraph wires by the State, and the wisdom of that important step has assuredly been amply proved during that period. Telegraphic resources have been developed to an enormous extent, and the great facilities which have been afforded to the public, the general extensions that have been made wherever they appeared to be desirable, the extension of the telephonic system (of which we shall presently speak), and other numerous improvements, all tend to prove the capacity and ability of the Post Office authorities for administering so important a system as that of the Telegraphs. That system has now, indeed, been brought into close connection with every relationship of life ; the wires have been brought to the very doors almost of every individual ; and people no longer hear with alarm the double knock of the telegraph-boy, for telegrams are sent and received now without the trepidation of former times. In short, the wires are not restricted to the uses of people engaged in speculative businesses, as was undoubtedly the case prior to the transfer, but are open to and are freely used by the whole population.

The great progress which has been made in telegraphic communication cannot, perhaps, be better demonstrated than by the following few comparative figures. The greatest number of messages telegraphed by the old companies in the course of a year never exceeded 1½ millions; now that number is sent in *a week*—over 78 millions of telegrams being transmitted in the course of a year. There are now about 10,000 offices open for telegraph business, as compared with 2932 under the companies; while the Post Office has close upon 30,000 instruments in use, whereas the companies only used 4000. The wires are now worked by the simplex, duplex, quadruplex, and even sextuplex systems, while the simplex was the only system known to the companies. The companies had 14,776 miles of line and 59,430 miles of wire, as compared with 32,881 miles of line and 206,304 miles of wire possessed by the Post Office. The number of words which could be transmitted in a minute on the fastest kind of instrument prior to the transfer was 70; now as many as 600 words can be sent in the same short space of time. The average charge for an ordinary inland telegram under the old rates was 2s. 2d.; now it is 7¾d. These statistics illustrate more forcibly than could otherwise be done the great advantages that have accrued since the Government acquired the electric systems of the country, and which have tended to make telegraphy an indispensable feature of modern life.

The chief or central Telegraph Station is, of course, at St. Martin's le Grand, being located in the General Post Office West. Formerly it was situated in a small street opening out of Moorgate Street, named Telegraph Street, from which the station has derived its code-signal of "T.S." The principal room of the station is perhaps the largest of its kind in the world, and occupies about 20,000 square feet, being provided with mahogany tables extending to about two-thirds

CENTRAL TELEGRAPH OFFICE, ST. MARTIN'S LE GRAND.

of a mile. The station is divided into different galleries, in each of which messages of a particular kind are dealt with. The total number of clerks employed in the Central Telegraph Station is 2911, of whom 869 are females, besides nearly 600 messengers. From 8 A.M. to 8 P.M. female clerks are chiefly employed, but from 8 P.M. to 8 A.M. only male clerks are employed. This large staff is managed by a Controller, one deputy, and three assistant controllers, while the comforts of the female staff are looked after by a matron.

TELEGRAPHIC OPERATING ROOM, CENTRAL TELEGRAPH OFFICE.

The work of this great telegraphic station is divided into two important classes, namely, that which deals with provincial and that which deals with metropolitan telegrams. The work of the former is technically known as the "sortation of messages." All messages received at the Central Telegraph Station for re-transmission have to be either sent to some part of London, or to some part of the country, or to some place abroad. If to some part of London, they are sent to the metropolitan gallery, or if abroad, to the foreign gallery or to the office of the Cable Company, by which they will be transmitted. Those messages intended for transmission to provincial places are sorted to one of the four great divisions in which the provincial circuits have been arranged, namely, circuits for the west and south-west of England and the Channel Islands; circuits for the east and south-east of England; circuits for the north and north-east of England and for Scotland; and circuits for the north-west of England, Ireland, and the Isle of Man. The control of each of these important divisions is entrusted to a woman clerk, a fact which redounds to the credit of the fair sex. The sorting table for messages received by tube from the collecting offices is subdivided into eight pans— namely, one for each of the four divisions mentioned, the fifth for the metropolitan gallery, the sixth for foreign telegrams, the seventh spare, and the eighth is termed a "blind" pan—that is to say, it is set apart for messages whose circulation is dubious. All messages passing in and out of the station are recorded and numbered at the sorting tables to which they may be conveyed; and they are also entered daily in an abstract in accurate numerical order; and again at the delivery table an account is made out every hour of the messages which are sent out for delivery during that period, being thus the means of letting the superintendent see whether the work is progressing at its proper speed or not.

All the circuits working into and out of the Central Telegraph Office are not only arranged geographically, but also all the circuits serving any one town or district are placed side by side; for instance, all the Liverpool circuits are placed together in one portion of the gallery, and all the Charing Cross or House of Commons circuits are together in another portion. The advantages of this system are that the clerks in charge can see at a glance whether the wires serving an important town or district are equally busy, and can make arrangements for feeding all circuits equally with messages. A similar system obtains at all the large offices in the kingdom. The metropolitan gallery, like the provincial gallery, is divided into six distinct sections, and the general arrangements are similar to those adopted in the provincial gallery, the same geographical position of the circuits being also observed.

As may be imagined, the Central Telegraph Office is fitted up with all the varieties of telegraphic instruments extant, but perhaps the most interesting is the Hughes type-printing instrument. Resembling a piano, having a key-board containing a number of black and white keys, this instrument has a large type-wheel made to rotate rapidly by means of pedal movement, and when a particular key is depressed, the message which is being transmitted is printed, simultaneously at the destination and office of origin, in clear Roman characters on narrow slips of paper which run out from the instruments at both ends of the circuit while being manipulated. The rapidity with which messages are sent on this instrument is marvellous. On one occasion, whilst inspecting the Central Telegraph Station, the clerk at the Hughes instrument, which communicated with Liverpool, in order to show the writer the truly beautiful working of the instrument, sent to that town as follows:— "Here visitors—please say what weather you have," which, of course, we saw being printed on the slip running from the instrument at one end ; and in less than one minute came the answer, being printed on the same slip (which was handed to us as a memento of the occasion), "Here very fine."

The Wheatstone automatic instrument is much used in the Central Telegraph Office. Its construction is also of an ingenious character, while its utility is invaluable on busy circuits, such as Leeds, Birmingham, etc. The messages for this instrument are first punched on strips of paper by two clerks, and then passed through the instrument, which at the other end of the circuit becomes printed in the Morse code of "dot" and "dash." A striking feature of usefulness in this instrument is that when the message is once punched out on the slip, the perforated tape or slip can, so long as it is kept whole, be used for any number of circuits over which the message may have to be transmitted, thereby saving much time and labour. Hence, as may be supposed, the instrument is chiefly used for the despatch of news and Press telegrams. The most simple of all the instruments in the Central Telegraph Station is Sir Charles Wheatstone's A.B.C. instrument, which is chiefly used for the private wire system.

H

The news branch forms a special feature of the
telegraphic service, the whole of the arrangements
connected therewith being controlled from headquarters by what is officially known as the Intelligence Department. A specially trained and skilled
staff of telegraphists is maintained for the express
purpose of working the wire over which news is
transmitted, not only in the London office, but also
all over the country wherever the importance of the
news to be telegraphed may demand their attendance. For, of course, news does not originate in
London alone. Events
are occurring in all parts
of the kingdom, such
as race-meetings, mur-
ders, strikes, ceremo-
nials, elections, etc., of
which the general pub-
lic are ever anxious to
have the earliest intelligence. As may be
supposed, a general elec-
tion throws an immense

WHEATSTONE TELEGRAPH INSTRUMENT.

amount of extra work on the telegraph clerk.
The whole nation awaits with impatient eager-
ness, as if it were a matter of life and death,
the issue of each election as it occurs. If much is
due to the smartness of the pressman in satisfying
the almost insatiable demand of the public for news
at such a time, it must also be remembered that without the aid and skill of the telegraphist this result
could not be achieved. Not only, too, is news work
arduous, but it has to be done often under pressure,
and frequently under peculiarly devised circumstances.

Thus, on one occasion, when the Autumn Manœuvres, which always give rise to a vast increase of telegraph business, were on, the telegraph instruments had to be fitted in a barber's shop, "to the no slight discomfiture," we are told, "of the rustic customers when they learnt that they could not be shaved until the manœuvres were over."

Again, at the Scott Centenary at Edinburgh, the telegraph clerks had to work in the ice-room adjoining the banquet-room, where the water was quite two inches deep, the masons being still engaged in breaking the blocks of ice. On another occasion at Lewes, on Guy Fawkes' Day, the telegraphist, who had come over specially from Brighton to wire a column and a-half of news for a newspaper correspondent, was pelted by the crowd with squibs and other fireworks through the Post Office window.

A recent and most interesting feat of telegraphy was the telegraphing of the Queen's Jubilee message to all parts of the Empire. As Her Majesty was about to pass to her carriage on her triumphal progress through London, she entered the telegraph room at Buckingham Palace, and there pressed a button which was electrically connected with St. Martin's le Grand. And it is of human interest to record that the dot which came out on the Morse paper as a result of the pressure of the button was immediately followed by two slight clicks which, according to the experts, indicated a certain amount of nervousness on the part of the aged Sovereign at that supreme moment in her illustrious career. These signals, received at seven minutes past eleven A.M., on the 22nd of June, 1897, were the Queen's commands to the telegraph officials to despatch the now famous and touching royal

message to her subjects throughout her vast Empire—
" From my heart I thank my people. May God bless
them." That was the simple and affecting message,
and in a few seconds the words were speeding over
land and under sea to some forty distant stations in
every part of the globe where now floats the Union
Jack. In two minutes the message had passed
Teheran on its way to the far East, to Simla, Singapore, Hong Kong, etc. Within sixteen minutes the
first reply, that from Ottawa, Canada's capital, was
waiting in Buckingham Palace for the Queen's return.
In less than two hours in most instances—long before
Her Majesty reached the Mansion House—replies
from the Cape, from Australia, from Singapore, from
Hong Kong, from the Gold Coast, and other Colonies
and dependencies, were received in London, and were
being prepared for presentation to the Queen on her
return to the Palace, whence she had despatched her
affectionate greeting to her people. Such is the most
historic feat that the telegraphic world has known.

It will serve to afford an idea of the use of the
telegraph in connection with the distribution of
" news" to state that over six millions such telegrams
are sent in the course of the year, while over seven
hundred million words are transmitted in the course
of the same period.

A useful aid to telegraphy is the Pneumatic Tube
system, a system very extensively made use of by the
Post Office for the wholesale conveyance, as it were,
of messages from one part of London to another.
There are no less than thirty-two such tubes at the
Central Telegraph Station, all of which are composed
of lead, excepting that between the Fleet Street and
West Strand Offices, which is made of iron. There

are two systems in use, that of Mr. Latimer Clark, which was used for some time before the transfer of the telegraphs, and that of Messrs. Siemens and Halske, of London and Berlin.   The tubes run in all directions in the E.C. and W.C. districts, and the stations therein are connected by a double tube, which forms a complete circuit, and has a column of air always passing through it, and which is moved either by pres-

AT THE PNEUMATIC TUBES.

sure or vacuum, or by both ; the diameter of the tube is three inches.   The double tube is like a pneumatic railway, having an "up" and a "down" line, and is worked on the railway block system, for which purpose it is fitted with Tyer's patent train signalling apparatus.

Many curious and remarkable incidents occur in connection with the telegraph department.   Imagine, for example, the astonishment of a butler who received a telegram from his master—a certain nobleman— asking him to send at once "ten bob," as he was "greatly in need of it." Of course the message had been wrongly transmitted, "ten bob" having originally been "tin box." Another amusing instance of erroneous transmission occurred in connection with one of the gatherings held periodically at Braemar, when a certain earl telegraphed to Edinburgh for a "cocked hat" to be sent him at once. In transmission the article mentioned as wanted was converted into "cooked ham," which was actually forwarded forthwith, greatly to the surprise and indignation, as may well be supposed, of the nobleman. A telegram once received was as follows :—"Please send your *pig* to meet me." Of course it should have been "gig," but the instrument made what is called a false dot, by recording . — — . (P.) instead of — — . (G.) Another story tells of a gentleman who, being detained out on business, telegraphed for his wife, but was strangely surprised to receive by the next train a *wig* instead. Another freak of wire! During the lectures by the Anti-Papist Murphy at Bury, Lancashire, he was severely handled by the mob, and according to a telegram "seven of the men charged with an assault on Mr. Murphy were *boiled* (bailed)." Such are a few instances of the pranks which the telegraph, either through inaccurate operating or through the perverseness of the current, will at times play, showing that like all things human the system is liable to err.

The transfer on the 4th of April, 1896, to the State of the trunk wires of the National Telephone Company is to be regarded as one of the most important events in the history of the Telephone service, as well as in that of the Post Office. The step is one which had long been contemplated, and took nearly four years in achievement. It is to be remembered, however, that the whole question was fraught with considerable difficulty to the Post Office. It is no part of the present history to deal with the invention or subsequent success of the telephone. Its utility and its necessity as an accessory of modern life are accepted facts, and it is only in its connection with the Post Office that we are now concerned. From the time of its introduction into general use until the date already mentioned, the telephone had been in the hands of a few companies. It having, however, been decided at law that a telephonic message was a telegram within the meaning of the Act, these companies have been under licence to the Post Office, paying an annual royalty, while it became the duty of the Government to take precautions to guard against an infringement of their monopoly of the telegraph system. But not only was this necessary; it was also essential that steps should be taken to prevent any one of the telephone companies, which were allowed to carry on their business under licence from the Government, obtaining a monopoly, not only to the exclusion of other companies, but also to the detriment of the public interests. This point was anxiously considered by the Post Office in 1884, when it was announced to Parliament that to avoid the bringing about of such a monopoly, it had been decided to invite competition from various quarters by granting licences to private companies. The desired result of this policy was not, however, in effect fulfilled, for one of the largest companies managed to rid itself of its rivals by buying most of them up, thereby going a long way towards constituting that monopoly which Parliament sought to prevent. The expiration of the patents, and the general dissatisfaction evinced by the public at the want of development of the telephonic system, forced the subject upon the attention of the Government, who accordingly undertook to look into the whole matter. It soon became apparent that the only satisfactory solution of the question was for the Post Office alone to possess the trunk wires between towns, and to co-operate with the companies in rendering additional services to the public. In arriving at this decision, the Government was, no doubt, influenced by the fact that under the then existing system the telegraph revenue was suffering seriously, as well as by the circumstance that the extension of telephones was being checked, to use the words of the Treasury minute on the subject, "in a manner which cannot be permanently maintained." It was upon that minute that the bill embodying the proposals of the Government as to the telephone service was subsequently introduced into Parliament, and became law under the title of the Telegraph Act, 1892.

Chief among the provisions of this Act is the purchase of the trunk lines of the companies, and the construction of a Government system to connect the business centres of the kingdom, and for this purpose it authorised the loan of a million sterling. Trunk lines have now been erected between various important centres, such as Glasgow and Belfast, Leeds and Hull, London and Brighton, etc. And the entire system when completed will consist of metallic circuits, and each of the towns connected will be able to communicate direct with London, or with each other.

Since the Telegraph Act of 1892 was passed the telephone companies have all passed out of existence, except the National Telephone Company, whose trunk wires have been, as already stated, transferred to the Crown. The matter was, as may be imagined, one of considerable difficulty, but an agreement was finally arrived at, with the result that the wires were purchased at a cost of £459,000 to the Post Office. By the transfer 200 trunk-line centres have been opened up at the principal towns in the country, 25,000 miles of telephone wires having thus been acquired, in addition to which 10,000 miles have been laid by the Department. In parting with the trunk wires the company has had its business restricted within defined local areas, where their exchanges are maintained ; but the local systems have been brought into communication with the trunk system by means of junction wires between the exchanges and the Post Offices. The junction wires can also be used by the public for transmitting messages to the Post Office, to be re-transmitted over the postal wires as ordinary telegrams, or to be conveyed and delivered by post as ordinary letters. These wires are also available for calling the services of Post Office express messengers, or for obtaining the delivery of telegrams by telephones, instead of in the ordinary manner, at places within the limit of the town.

The charges for using the trunk wires between the places which are connected, are according to distance, the rates being 3d. for any distance of twenty miles or under ; 6d. for any distance over twenty miles, and not over forty miles; and 6d. for every additional forty miles. The 6d. rate had been in operation for the trunk wires already provided by the Post Office, but the 3d. rate was introduced with the transfer, the Government considering that there should be this lower charge for the short wires. Longer distances, it seems, cannot be charged for at a less rate, for although the terminal expenses are a fixed quantity, the expenses of construction and maintenance increase greatly, even in proportion, with the length of the line. Where a submarine cable is used, or where exceptional expense is incurred, additional charges will be made. The period of conversation is, as in the case of the London-Paris telephone, restricted to three minutes, and two consecutive periods are allowed for a double payment.

There can be no question that the acquisition by the State of the trunk telephone wires is a step by which the nation must benefit in the future. Facilities for telephonic communication will be developed, not only by the more widely extended system, but also by the fact that the public are able now to telephone at about one-half the rates charged by the companies. The restriction to oral communications, too, under which the companies laboured, being removed, and the system being brought into conjunction with the post-letter and telegraph services of the Post Office, enhances the value of telephonic communication to an almost unlimited degree. There can be no doubt that the future of the telephone service in this country offers a prospect of great development and of much increased utility and advantage to the community.

CHAPTER IX.

THE ADMINISTRATION AND STAFF.

ALTHOUGH the machinery of the Post Office is simple enough, the organisation of the department is very vast and complex. As at present constituted the British Post Office has, with a few exceptions, an exclusive authority to convey letters within the United Kingdom. It is also required to convey newspapers; and it undertakes the conveyance of parcels, books, and the remittance of small sums of money; it also engages in savings bank, life insurance and annuity business; and it likewise has an exclusive right of telegraphic business. It is only, however, as regards letters and telegrams that the Post Office possesses any privilege, the other branches of its business being open to any persons who may choose to undertake them.

By means of the railways, and of steam-boats, mail-coaches, stage-coaches, mail-carts, mounted and foot messengers, letters and other postal packets are despatched and received daily in all parts of the country. In many cases, including all important towns, the communication is twice a-day or oftener. Mails are also despatched by packets or private ships to all parts of the globe.

The supreme head of the vast organisation of the

Post Office is the Postmaster-General, who, subject to the provisions of the law, and to the controlling authority of the Lords of the Treasury, has the direction of all postal affairs within the United Kingdom.   In the United Kingdom, the Lords of the Treasury have power, within limits prescribed by law, to fix the rates of postage; and the Postmaster-General has authority to determine the frequency and speed with which the mails shall be conveyed and letters delivered.   The office of Postmaster-General was established by the Act 9 Anne, cap. 10, under the provisions of which the whole of the Post Office was to be "under the control of an officer who shall be appointed by the Queen's Majesty, her heirs and successors, to be made and constituted by letters patent under the Great Seal, by the name and style of Her Majesty's Postmaster-General."   On one occasion, as we have seen, the office was held jointly by two persons.   This was in the reign of William III., and on the accession of Queen Anne the office was continued to the same two chiefs, who divided the salary between them.   This system of dual control was, with two or three exceptions, continued down to 1823, when it was abolished.   Since then the supreme control of the Post Office has been vested in one person, who is either a member of the House of Lords or the House of Commons, and is frequently of Cabinet rank in the Ministry.   His salary is £2500 a-year, and he is, of course, responsible to Parliament and the Nation for the welfare of the Post Office, and he has the power to make promotions and appointments within his department; he has also the power of dismissal; and he has in his gift all postmasterships in England and Wales as well as in Scotland and

Ireland. As is known, of course, a new Postmaster-General is appointed with every change of Government.

The chief permanent official is the Secretary, who is in receipt of a salary of £1750, which after five years' service is increased to £2000. He is the responsible adviser of the Postmaster-General, and the principal administrator of the Department. He is assisted by a Second Secretary whose salary is £1250, and after three years £1400, and six Assistant Secretaries whose salaries are £1000, and after five years £1200. These officials are of course responsible for various sections of the Post Office work, and assist in advising the Postmaster-General. The Secretary's Office is the controlling department of the Post Office: it is the medium of communication with the Government through the Treasury, and it is also the medium of communication between the subordinate departments and the Postmaster-General. It of course exercises control over all provincial offices, and most of the correspondence with the public is carried on here, while the various arrangements for the well-working of the service are decided upon in the Secretary's Office. The present staff of the Secretary's Office, including the Postal Stores Department, numbers over 700 persons, of whom nine are principal clerks with a maximum salary each of £800 a-year, and one controller (Postal Stores) with a maximum salary of £700.

The Solicitor's Office deals of course with all the legal questions arising out of Post Office work. The Solicitor enjoys a maximum salary of £2000 a-year, and his assistant £1000 a-year, besides whom there are nine other officials of various grades.

The Accountant-General's Department is controlled by the Comptroller and Accountant-General, who is the responsible adviser of the Postmaster-General on all Post Office financial matters. The post is an onerous, as well as a responsible one, from the complex nature of the duties pertaining to it, and the holder takes equal rank with the Second Secretary and enjoys a similar scale of salary—viz., £1250, and after three years £1400. The work of the Accountant-General's Department, as may be supposed, deals with the various Post Office accounts ; it involves the examination of the daily cash accounts and periodical revenue accounts rendered by the various postmasters throughout England and Wales, and the keeping of the accounts of revenue and expenditure. It also pays all salaries, pensions, and items of expenditure. This office also deals with the various telegraph accounts, both inland and foreign, while to it is attached the Postal Order Branch, which deals with the examination and disposal of all paid postal orders, and the supplies of postal orders to postmasters. This branch is entirely composed of women clerks and sorters, of whom there are 438 altogether. A portion of the telegraph work is also performed by women clerks, of whom there are 198 employed in what is known as the Clearing-House Branch. The importance of the Accountant-General's Department will be realised when it is stated that the annual revenue, with the collection of which it is charged, amounts to £14,640,000, while the expenditure with which it has to deal is at the rate of £11,000,000 a-year. The total staff required to cope with the work of this large department now numbers about 1900 persons, of whom one is Assistant Accountant-

General, 4 principal Staff-Officers, 12 Accountants, 13 Assistant Accountants, and 22 Examiners.

The London Postal Service is one of the most important departments, as has already been seen from the glimpse of the work which was given in a former chapter. The whole staff comprises over 13,000 persons, but that, of course, includes all the London District Offices. There is in addition an unestablished force of nearly 6000 persons. At the General Post Office East there is a Controller, with a maximum salary of £1200 a-year; a Vice-Controller, with £850 a-year; two Assistant-Controllers, and six Superintendents.

The Money Order Office is, as the name implies, the controlling centre of Money Order business, of which we shall speak in the next chapter. Its staff comprises 220 persons, of whom one is Controller, with a maximum salary of £900 a-year, one Assistant-Controller, and three Principal Clerks.

The Returned Letter Office, which deals with undelivered letters, has a staff of 134 persons, of whom one is Controller, with a maximum salary of £650 a-year. Female Returners, to the number of fifty-one, are included in the staff of this Office.

The Savings Bank Department, which is located in Queen Victoria Street, employs a huge staff, as may be inferred from the gigantic nature of its transactions, of which we shall also speak in the following chapter. This Office is, of course, the administrative centre of Savings Bank business, and keeps a personal account with every depositor, of whom there are about 6,500,000. It acknowledges the receipt of every single deposit, and sends out all withdrawal notices. Each year the savings bank-book of each depositor is sent here for examination, and at the same time interest is calculated and allowed. This Office also manages the correspondence with the public and the postmasters arising out of savings bank business. The staff of the Savings Bank Department comprises over 2000 persons, of whom 850 are females. There are, one Controller, with a maximum salary of £1000 a-year, two Assistant-Controllers, and four Sub-Controllers.

Among the minor departments in London may be mentioned the Medical Department, comprising four-

GENERAL POST OFFICE, EDINBURGH.

teen persons, of whom one is chief medical officer, with a maximum salary of £1000; and the House-keeping Department, which employs 129 persons.

So far, we have only spoken of the London establishment, but, as may be imagined, an extraordinarily large provincial establishment has to be maintained. Both at Edinburgh and Dublin there are Administrative Offices, from which the postal arrangements in Scotland and Ireland are controlled, each country boasting of a Secretary, with a maximum salary of

£1200 a-year. There are, of course, Secretary's Offices, Accountant's, Solicitor's, Sorting, and Returned Letter Offices, as in London, but on a miniature scale. While, however, the control of the Scotch and Irish postal business is vested in the respective Secretaries, these officials are directly responsible to the authorities in London for all branches of Post Office work.

An important link between the Provincial Establishments and the Metropolitan Offices is the Surveying Department. At the present time there are sixteen Surveyors, each of whom receives a maximum salary of £800 a-year, and each having an Assistant-Surveyor, whose maximum annual salary is £500. The whole Surveying staff consists of 180 persons, of whom 126 are clerks, and the cost of the staff, including travelling expenses, amounts to nearly £68,000 a-year. Each surveyor is responsible for a certain district of the country, and it is his duty to supervise the various Post Offices throughout that district, and he is responsible for the efficient working and discipline of the respective staffs of those offices. The surveyor has to visit periodically each office in his district, to remedy where he can all defects in the working of the postal system; to remove, when possible, all just grounds of complaint on the part of the public ; to check the accounts ; to give the correspondence of the district increased celerity, regularity, and security when opportunity offers, and to arrange for contracts with these objects. The Act of Queen Anne provided for the appointment of one surveyor to the Post Office, whose duty it should be to make proper surveys of post roads. Now, as has been seen, the service necessitates the employment of sixteen

I

surveyors, besides whom several of the more important postmasters act as their own surveyors.

The postmasters with whom the surveyors have to
deal are a large and comprehensive body, there being
now as many as 900 head postmasters and 18,000
sub-postmasters through the United Kingdom. These
offices, of course, vary in importance, according to
the size of the towns in which they are situated, and
the salaries of the postmasters range from £1000
a-year downwards. The duties of a postmaster
nowadays are both onerous and responsible—very
different from the days before the Post Office had
taken over and absorbed other branches of business.
He must not only have a complete knowledge of
postal work proper and the town for which he is
responsible, but he must be fully acquainted with
telegraph work, money order and savings bank business, as well as life insurance and annuity work, and
Parcel Post duties. He has to render, daily and
weekly, a variety of accounts to the Metropolitan
Office, and is responsible for his cash balance, to
which end he is placed under bond, so that the
Government is fairly free from losses under this head.

Speaking of this system the Postmaster-General
remarks, in one of his annual reports, that "owing
to the successful measures which the Department has
adopted by means of bonds, frequent supervision,
and care in the selection of persons admitted into the
service, and afterwards promoted therein, very few
losses have occurred through defalcation. More than
twenty years ago, however, a postmaster who owed
the Office £2000, but who had given security for only
a part of that sum, absconded, leaving an unpaid debt
of upwards of £1000. The recovery of the debt had

long been considered hopeless, but a short time ago a letter was unexpectedly received from the post-master's son enclosing a remittance in payment of part of his father's debt, and expressing a hope that after a time he should be able to pay the remainder—a hope which was soon realised, every farthing of the debt having been discharged, in a manner most creditable to the gentleman concerned."

Every head postmaster is, of course, directly re-sponsible for the full efficiency and proper manage-ment of his office, and under the approval of his surveyor, the sanction of the Postmaster-General, and the favourable report of the Civil Service Commission-ers, he is allowed to appoint nearly the whole of his own officers, he being responsible to the authorities for their proper discipline and good conduct. As may be imagined, an enormous staff has to be employed at the various Post Offices throughout the country in carry-ing on the business of the Department, and the number now employed is considerably over 45,000, of whom quite 13,000 are engaged on clerical duties.

The staff of the whole Post Office would form quite a respectable army, numbering as it does at the present time 140,806 persons, of whom 79,235 are borne on the permanent establishment. Of the latter number 11,857 are women, while of the 61,571 persons who are not on the permanent establishment the number of women is about 16,300, thus making a total of over 28,000 situations in the Post Office which are filled by women. Of that number, as already indicated, a large proportion are engaged upon actual clerical duties by ladies of good social position. The employment of women as clerks is a movement in which the Post Office was one of the pioneers. The experiment of employing ladies to do actual clerk-work was first tried by the Post Office as far back as 1871, and so soon showed such favourable results that it was greatly extended. After a trial of some three or four years the scheme was found to be so markedly successful that it was rapidly and widely developed, and, as has been seen, lady clerks are now employed in various branches of the Post Office to the number of over 1200, that number excluding some 400 female sorters. The favourable results that have attended the Post Office scheme of employing female clerks have led to their employment to a considerable extent in outside offices, for the experience of the Post Office has shown that ladies enjoying good health, and of tolerable education and abilities, are quite fitted to fulfil the duties of less responsible clerkships, while not a few are quite competent to occupy positions of trust, responsibility, and even in some cases of an administrative character.

The employment of so enormous a staff as has been shown above, is only maintained at a large cost to the Department. The amount annually expended at the present time is at the rate of £6,629,774, or over 45 per cent. of the total revenue earned in the year by the Post Office, and over 60 per cent. of its total yearly expenditure.

The provision which has to be made for the accommodation of the huge staff of the Post Office is likewise on an extensive scale. Without doubt the Post Office of the present time is one of the vastest institutions that exist in this country, for it penetrates in some shape or form to every town, village or hamlet; to small out-of-the-way places where even the railway is as yet an unknown accessory of local life—in short, to every inhabited nook and corner of the United Kingdom.

There are at the present time about 21,000 Post Offices throughout the country.   Of course these offices vary considerably according to the population of the district in which they are situated, ranging from the mammoth piles at St. Martin's le Grand, and the palatial offices of such towns as Liverpool, Manchester, Birmingham, and Glasgow, down to the humble abode of the village disciple of St. Crispin, who, in the intervals that he is not cobbling his neighbours' shoes, attends to their wants in matters postal. So rapidly, however, is Post Office business growing in all its branches, that handsome edifices are springing up with mushroom-like growth throughout the land, and the quaint, crazy old offices which were wont to delight the holiday tourist are fast disappearing, while the old-fashioned window-office, which some of us can still just remember, is almost a thing of the past.   The local Post Office in any town of importance is now a more or less pretentious landmark, while the interior is fitted up with handsome fittings and furniture, with a view to the comfort of the public who have postal business to transact, and of the staff who have to perform the varied duties connected with the office.

The most interesting feature of the local Post Office to the stranger is, of course, the sorting-room, which is usually a spacious apartment lying immediately at the back of the public counter, being furnished with rows of sorting-tables, and every modern appliance for dealing with the correspondence that passes through the office.   Peeping into one of these sorting-rooms in the daytime, we should find it almost desolate both of work and workers, from which, no doubt, the uninitiated would conclude that the lot of the provincial Post Office clerk was not altogether an unhappy one. Let such an one, however, penetrate to this same room at midnight or thereabouts, and he shall find a complete transformation of scene. A crowd of busy, eager workers will be discovered, immersed in letters, newspapers, parcels, and postal packets of every imaginable description, which are being sorted, stamped, bagged, and otherwise dealt with, so as to attain the great end of making up the night mails. The true home of letters is, of course, to be found at St. Martin's le Grand, the fountain-head of our great postal system. In a previous chapter we have given some idea of the enormous quantity of business transacted nightly there.

The acquisition of sites and buildings is an important item in Post Office expenditure, and varies, of course, from year to year. Last year, we are told, the expenditure under this head amounted to £67,000, of which £32,000 was spent in London. It should be explained, perhaps, that the cost of erecting and furnishing new buildings, as well as the maintenance and enlargement of existing buildings, falls upon the Office of Works, and the amount thus expended during the course of last year was £305,000 in Great Britain, and £8300 in Ireland.

CHAPTER X.

THE POST OFFICE OF TO-DAY.

THE Post Office has grown so rapidly in recent years, and has become so indissolubly connected with our daily life, that its huge dimensions and unlimited convenience have almost ceased to be a marvel. Yet, when one calmly considers the gigantic character of the business done, the rapidity and regularity with which its services are performed, and the smoothness with which the vast and complex machinery of the department works year in and year out, we are forced to the conclusion that the Post Office of to-day is one of the wonders of the world.

There can, of course, be no doubt that without the railways the Post Office could never have been what it is. However inconvenient the high postal rates and imperfect arrangements of former days were, the inconvenience was not felt acutely until the introduction of the railways rendered locomotion throughout the country a simpler and cheaper matter than it had hitherto been. For the dis-uniting of families was an early result of railway travelling, and relations and friends who began to be scattered far and wide soon realised a distinct hardship in the circumstance that, owing to the expensiveness of the

post, correspondence could only be carried on at rare
intervals.   The late Sir Rowland Hill himself is said
to have had this hardship forcibly borne in upon him
by the fact that when engaged to his future wife he
and she found it necessary, from motives of economy,
to sacrifice sentiment and to restrict their correspondence to one letter a-fortnight.   What influence the
circumstance may have had in determining the great
postal reform of 1840, it would be idle to conjecture,
but there can be no doubt that the subsequent
development of the idea of uniform Penny Postage
into one of the greatest social reforms of the century
has earned for Rowland Hill the gratitude and good-
will of all posterity.

Truly, the fifty and odd years that have elapsed
since the introduction of uniform penny postage in
this country have effected a wondrous revolution in
our postal system.   In 1839 seventy-six million letters were carried by the post, a number that standing
alone seems imposing enough, and of which the
Postmaster-General of that day was, no doubt, reason-
ably proud when he compared the figures with those
of by-gone years.   But compare them with the enormous number carried at the present time and they
sink into utter insignificance.   That number is at the
rate of over 1,834,000,000 in the year, which works out
to an average of forty-six letters to each individual
of the population.   Book packets, circulars, and
samples are sent at the rate of 672,300,000 in the
year, and newspapers at the rate of 149,000,000
annually.   Post cards, which were first introduced in
1870, are also used to an enormous extent, as may be
judged by the fact that 314,500,000 are delivered in
the course of the year.   Then there is the Parcel Post

system, introduced in 1883, under which 60,327,000 parcels are posted annually. If these various figures be lumped together it will be found that the Post Office at the present time has to carry and deliver the fabulous number of over 3000 million packets in the course of a year. This is, indeed, a brilliant record ! The letter statistics alone are a marvellous testimony to the unqualified success of the postal reform of 1840.

Viewing the matter at this distant date and enjoying, as we do, to the full the benefits conferred by that scheme, it is certainly hard to believe that so much opposition and resistance were at first made to the proposition. It seems, however, to be the inevitable fate of all innovations and schemes for improvement to be met with distrust and suspicion, and when Sir Rowland Hill had to prove his opinions, to struggle for a trial of his plans, and to meet the host of objections and obstacles placed in his path, he but passed through the ordeal which all reformers, before and since, have, more or less, had to undergo. It must have been a great triumph for the reformer to have been spared to see his calculations and predictions realised so immensely beyond his own expectations.

A most useful development of the letter post is the Registered Letter system, by which small articles of value can be transmitted through the post. The subject was one which received much attention at the hands of Rowland Hill, prior to whose time the fee for the registration of letters had been excessive. The matter has always been one of considerable importance, for it is essential that letters which contain coin or valuables passing through the post should, as far as possible, be insured against risk of loss or theft. On the other hand it is equally desirable to remove, by the system pursued in dealing with registered letters, the temptation to evil into which the handling of such letters might lead those who have to deal with them. Prior to 1840 every letter supposed to contain articles of value was registered, but this practice was abandoned owing to the constantly increasing pressure arising out of the rapid growth of letter business after the introduction of Penny Postage. But the change of practice led to numerous complaints of theft from the public, and other difficulties speedily arose. The Post Office authorities then proposed a system under which one shilling should be charged for country registered letters, and twopence for district post letters. Rowland Hill opposed the scheme, and desired to introduce a uniform sixpenny rate, but, although he then held his Treasury appointment, his influence was so small that he had to give way so far as to agree to a uniform shilling rate. This difference of opinion on the part of Rowland Hill, it is interesting to note, was the indirect cause of his subsequent removal from the Treasury in 1842, for he had, it appears, crossed with his advice a strong wish of Lord Lowther's, the then Postmaster-General—a circumstance that was neither forgotten nor forgiven. On Rowland Hill's recall to office, some few years later, he promptly introduced the sixpenny rate for registered letters, a boon that was greatly appreciated at the time.

This rate was subsequently reduced to fourpence, and on the 1st of January, 1878, to twopence, a circumstance which, coupled with the facilities now afforded to the public for sending registered letters by the sale of envelopes specially devised for the purpose, and the comparatively high scale of money-order commission, soon caused a huge increase in the number of such letters.

In the first year after the reduction of the fee to twopence, considerably more than 7 millions such letters were sent through the post in the United Kingdom, being nearly double the number posted in the previous year. The number sent at the present time is at the rate of over 13 millions in the year, and the number would no doubt have been much greater but for the immense popularity of the Postal Order system, of which we shall presently speak. Notwithstanding the cheap registration fee, there are still persons who, either for the sake of saving a few pence or of cheating the revenue, appear to be unable to divest themselves of the propensity of transmitting through the post, without the precaution of registration, articles which ought clearly to be registered. It is curious what devices are sometimes resorted to for this purpose. A Bank of England note for £20 found pinned to the page of a book addressed to the initials of a lady at a Post Office in the metropolis, and a halfpenny wrapper containing, besides a letter, a bill of sale and four Bank of England notes, are but two instances out of many annually coming under the notice of the Post Office, without taking into account those that pass undetected.

A peculiar trait in the character of the public is also exhibited by the fact that the authorities are in constant receipt of applications for missing registered letters, which, in most cases, on inquiries being made, are found either never to have been posted at all or to have been mislaid and their delivery forgotten. In one case, a number of Suez Canal Shares, which were applied for as missing, were found in the addressee's waste-paper basket, where they had been thrown under the impression that they were circulars; and, in another instance, a letter containing bank notes, said to have been registered, was discovered behind a desk in the sender's office. Needless to remark, the rashness in jumping to conclusions in this respect by the public is apt to hamper and harass the Post Office officials in their already onerous and numerous duties. It will further illustrate the want of care displayed by the public in regard to letters of all kinds, to state that last year 31,879 letters were posted without any address at all, and of that number 2133 contained property to the value of £3860. In addition, 6462 parcels were also received without any address. The total number of returned packets dealt with in the Returned Letter Office (formerly known as the Dead Letter Office) last year was about 18 millions. The value of the property found in the letters which were opened in that Office exceeded £580,000, and, in addition to these, many registered letters, having the name and address of the sender written outside, were returned unopened.

One of the most important developments of our postal system in modern times is undoubtedly the introduction of the Parcel Post on the 1st of August, 1883. The question of initiating such a system had long been agitating many minds, and was broached, indeed, so far back as 1842. The opposition of the railway companies was, however, a constant obstacle, as it continued to be in later years. The question was brought forward at a special meeting of the Society of Arts in 1858, at which Earl Fortescue —then Lord Ebington—took the chair. An able report was drawn up and adopted by the Society, recommending that the Post Office should convey parcels at moderate charges, irrespective of distance ; but although carefully considered by the postal authorities, nothing practical resulted. Mr. Edwin Chadwick also took the matter in hand some years later, but with no better result. Chief among more recent advocates of the reform was the late Professor Jevons, whose authority in all financial matters of course lent great weight to his arguments. The difficulties which apparently lay in the way of a State Parcel Post being established were apparently very great, and it was not until the late Mr. Fawcett, when he was Postmaster-General, took up the question that they were overcome. The necessary Act was passed in 1882, and a year later the new service was in operation.

More than fourteen years have elapsed since the Parcel Post was established, and the progress of the business, on the whole, appears to have been very satisfactory. At first, of course, there were many little defects and shortcomings, but it only required a short experience to show where modification and reform were needed. The most satisfactory statistics are now on record as to this business. Thus, the total number of parcels now posted in a year is at the rate of over 60 millions, the number of registered parcels being at the rate of 700,000. When the system was first introduced, the charges were as follows :—3d. for 1 lb. and under, 6d. from 1 lb. up to 3 lbs., 9d. from 3 lbs. up to 5 lbs., and 1s. from 5 lbs. up to 7 lbs.; but these rates were revised in May, 1885, by which the postage was fixed at a minimum of 3d., increasing by 1½d. per lb., to a maximum of 1s. 6d. for 11 lbs. Quite recently a further revision has taken place, under which the rate increases from 3d. by a 1d. per lb. instead of 1½d.

In July, 1885, a Foreign and Colonial Parcel Post was inaugurated, and the system has since been extended to all the colonies, except Queensland, and to almost all foreign countries. The number of parcels sent in the year between Great Britain and foreign and colonial states, in both directions, is at the rate of 1,800,000. The number of outgoing parcels to incoming ones is in the proportion of more than 2 to 1. The greatest amount of parcel business is done with France, Germany, Italy, and South Africa. The value of the goods exported and imported by Parcel Post last year was respectively £1,437,312 and £1,009,022. The total number of foreign and colonial parcels insured was 73,789. Many of the parcels are of great value, and sometimes contain between £2000 and £3000 in gold.

It is interesting to notice in connection with the Parcel Post Service that the Post Office has, in many instances, reverted to the coach services, and parcel coaches or vans run nightly between London and Brighton, Oxford, Chatham, Tunbridge Wells, Ipswich, Watford, and Hertford, and also between Liverpool and Manchester. This is a less expensive mode of conveyance than by railway, because the railway companies claim 55 per cent. of all the postage collected on parcels conveyed during any portion of the journey by rail.

A considerable impetus was given to the Inland Parcel Post by the introduction, in 1885, of a system of insurance and of compensation for loss or damage, under which compensation not exceeding £1 is now given where no insurance fee is paid ; and where an

THE BRIGHTON PARCEL COACH.

insurance fee of one penny or twopence is paid, compensation is given to the amount of £5 or £10. The plan is one which has fully commended itself to the public, as the annual number of registered parcels already stated indicates.

The Remittance Branch is one of the most important and useful adjuncts of the postal system. Sums of money can now be remitted through the post either by Money Order or Postal Order, the maximum limit in the former case being £10, and in the latter £1. The former service is the older, and dates back as far as 1838, when the business was carried on by three clerks in a couple of rooms at the north end of the old General Post Office, and one cannot but be impressed with the astonishing results that have since accrued.

At the very outset, when the Money Order Service was a purely private undertaking conducted by three enterprising individuals who happened to be engaged in the Post Office, the principle and utility of the system were at once seen and admitted, although the high rates of commission which, from various causes it was necessary to charge, restricted the usefulness of the service, and to a great extent rendered it prohibitive. As soon, however, as the charges were reduced, on the system passing over to the Government, the business immediately expanded, and a considerable increase at once took place in the number and amount of the transactions— an increase that was rapidly progressive year by year, and which, with each successive reduction in the scale of commission, was further greatly augmented. In 1871, when the initial rate was reduced to one penny for orders of 10s. and under, and the

K

whole scale based on the uniformity of the postage
rates, rising by gradations of one penny to a shilling,
the increase in the number and amount of Money
Orders was something enormous, being as regards the
number nearly 3,000,000, and as regards the amount,
more than £2,000,000 more than the preceding year.

But from a financial point of view the reduction
proved somewhat unfortunate, for the revenue from
this important branch of the Post Office began very
perceptibly to fall off. Every Money Order issued
and paid is estimated to cost the department on an
average threepence, and it therefore followed that on
the introduction of the penny initial rate, those orders
on which the commission was only a penny or twopence were devoid of profit. So serious indeed was
this circumstance that it soon became a source of
anxiety to the Government, who, after full consideration of the subject, found it absolutely necessary
to take precautionary steps by raising the initial rate
from a penny to twopence (as was done on the
1st of January, 1878), with a view to avoid a deficiency
that had hitherto only been averted through the
profits yielded by the Foreign and Colonial Money
Order business in conjunction with those from the
larger inland money orders.

Retrograde as this step was, there was no disput-
ing its wisdom, and it was considered by some, indeed,
a question whether the old threepenny rate ought
not to have been reverted to, as was suggested by
Mr. Chetwynd, C.B., of the Post Office, whose forty
years' direct and indirect experience of the Money
Order Office constituted him the very best authority on the subject. As it was, the authorities had
in view a scheme which, while it was to offer the

public a substitute for the loss of the old penny Money Order rate, would in operation displace the profitless money orders. Although the measure, which provided for a system of Postal Orders devised by Mr. Chetwynd, had been introduced into Parliament on more than one occasion, it was not until the year 1880 that it became duly legalised under the "Post Office (Money Orders) Act" of that year, considerable opposition having been offered by the banking community, who considered that such a system would seriously affect the currency question. These fears were, however, allayed, and with some few modifications the measure came into operation on the 1st of January, 1881.

Postal Orders are now issued for fourteen denominations, namely — 1s., 1s. 6d., 2s., 2s. 6d., 3s., 3s. 6d., 4s., 4s. 6d., 5s., 7s. 6d., 10s., 10s. 6d., 15s., and 20s.; at a commission of one-halfpenny for each of the two first amounts, a penny for each of the next ten, and three-halfpence for each of the remaining two classes. When first issued, the Postal Order is payable to bearer at any Money Order Office in the United Kingdom, but the Act requires that the purchaser shall insert the name of the payee, and that the payee shall insert the name of the Money Order Office (if that has not already been done by the sender) at which he desires to get it cashed. The remitter may also cross the Order generally or specifically so as to invest it with the advantages and safeguards of a cheque similarly dealt with. The period of circulation for postal orders is restricted to three months, after which they are only renewable upon payment of a commission equal to the amount of the original poundage for every three months that have elapsed after the month of issue.

The results of this new business have been almost phenomenal, and have entirely negatived the unfavourable predictions that the measure was subjected to. Postal Orders are now being sold at the enormous rate of over 64 millions a-year, to the value of nearly £24,000,000. Since the commencement of the business more than 563 million Postal Orders have been sold, to the value of over £220,000,000. These astonishing figures plainly show that the public thoroughly appreciate the convenience which this mode of remitting small sums by post has provided, and also that the anticipation of the benefits which it would confer have been amply justified.

The Money Order system still remains in operation, of course, as hitherto, and the rates have recently again been revised and simplified, so that the business is hardly affected beyond being relieved, as was intended, of those Orders for small amounts which are of no profit to the Department. The total number of inland Money Orders now issued, is at the rate of about ten millions in the year, to the value of nearly £26,000,000.

In the Savings Bank Department we have one of the brightest chapters in Post Office history. In viewing the results accomplished in this popular Department it is seen how much has been done by the Government to foster and encourage thrift among the poorer classes of the country. The subject has always been a generally interesting one, and the desirability of the Government assuming the custodianship of the savings of the poor was foreseen

and advocated long before the idea was reduced to
practical form. So early as 1807, a bill to legislate
on the subject was brought into Parliament by
Mr. Whitbread, but was subsequently withdrawn
owing to its impracticability. In 1860 the matter
was again revived by Mr. Sykes, a bank manager in
Huddersfield, who submitted a plan for the purpose
of utilising the existing money order offices for
savings bank business, which, while the principle of
it was seen to be useful, was, however, so crude, and
possessed such drawbacks, that it could not be acted
on. It was Mr. Chetwynd, at that time employed in
the Money Order office, who developed the idea and
brought it to a practicable and successful issue. His
plan was based upon the principle that savings bank
business might be done "through the various money
order offices in a much more economical manner than
by the issue and payment of money orders," as had
been suggested by Mr. Sykes, and he also proposed
that it should be so comprehensive as to dispense
with the pound restriction (also part of Mr. Sykes's
proposal), which he considered to be "so large as to
seriously reduce the value of the benefit proposed to
be conferred on the provident portion of the public."

The whole proposal, from its clearness and complete-
ness on every point of detail, at once commanded the
favourable attention of the Postmaster-General, and
speedily fell into the hands of Mr. Gladstone—then
Chancellor of the Exchequer—who, with his charac-
teristic energy and spirit, lost no time in introducing a
bill on the subject into the House of Commons ; and
on the 17th of May, 1861, the measure became law.

There was not wanting, of course, the usual amount
of opposition to the scheme, but the groundless

character of the objections raised was conclusively proved by the immediate success that attended the new system of Government Savings Banks. The *Times*, in September, 1861, testified to this gratifying result as follows :—"The country," wrote the leading journal, "soon recognised the universal boon of a bank maintained at the public responsibility, with the whole empire for its capital, with a branch in every town, open at almost all hours, and, more than all, giving a fair amount of interest."

The development of the system, since the date when the business was commenced with a staff of twenty clerks in a moderately-sized room in the old General Post Office East, has been marvellously rapid, and the number of deposits made continues to increase year by year. The number of deposits made in the year at the present time is at the rate of over eleven millions, amounting to more than £32,000,000, while the withdrawals number about four millions, amounting to about £25,000,000. The amount due to depositors in the Post Office Savings Banks is considerably more than £98,000,000. The average number of deposits made daily is over 37,000. It will be seen from the foregoing figures that the deposits exceed the withdrawals in amount to a considerable extent, a circumstance which of course is to be regarded with satisfaction.

The great success which attended this business led to facilities being afforded through the medium of the Post Office Savings Bank for the purchase and sale of Government stock in small sums. This was done under the Savings Bank Act of 1880, which gives power to depositors in Trustee and Post Office Savings Banks to invest any part of their deposits within prescribed limits in Government stock, through the agency of the Post Office, at a trifling cost, varying from 9d. to 2s. 3d., the dividends being collected free of any further charge. The limits are £200 in one year and £500 in all, these being, of course, irrespective of the limits for ordinary deposits. The investment can be effected either by a transfer from a depositor's account or by means of sums specially deposited for immediate investment. The system has been quite successful, and the purchase of stock in the last recorded year amounted to £1,112,568, while the sales amounted to £1,163,930. The amount of stock remaining to the credit of stockholders is about £7,000,000.

The minimum limit of deposit in the Post Office Savings Bank is, as is known, one shilling, but it was long urged that penny deposits should be received with the object of making the limit sufficiently low to reach the poorest classes. When the Savings Bank Act of 1880 was in Committee an amendment was proposed with the object of reducing the shilling limit accordingly. The system of the Post Office Savings Bank, however, rendered such a plan impracticable, especially in view of the high average cost of each transaction. The authorities were at the same time anxious to meet popular views, and decided upon bringing into operation a plan which, while it would not involve any actual relaxation of the shilling limit, would have the effect of practically fulfilling the same end. That plan was the Postage Stamp Savings Scheme, which has been in operation now for seventeen years with the utmost success. The plan enables poor persons desirous of saving to collect by means of penny stamps a shilling for deposit in the Postal Savings Bank. The stamps are affixed as collected to specially prepared slips supplied gratuitously at any Post Office. They must not, of course, be defaced or in any way damaged or mutilated. The extreme simplicity of the scheme, which is another of the late Mr. Chetwynd's inventions, is its great merit ; and, although it was at first objected that it would afford an opening for the disposal of stolen stamps, experience has shown that no serious risk in this respect need be feared.

The results of the scheme have proved most gratifying, both to the postal authorities as repaying their efforts to encourage providence by creating an opening for the saving of the smallest sums, and to the public in dispelling in a great measure a notion hitherto generally entertained, that the poorest classes of this country lack the faculty for saving, even if afforded the facilities for so doing.

The Post Office, determined to shut out no opening which may serve to encourage the habit of saving, is constantly offering fresh facilities for the convenience of depositors. After the Free Education Act was passed, arrangements were made whereby part of the saved school fees might be collected at the schools by the use of stamp slips, the attendance of the children and others at a distant savings bank being rendered unnecessary, a plan that has been taken much advantage of by the persons for whom it was intended. Navvies, too, employed on the construction of public works are afforded, at the place where they receive their wages, the opportunity of depositing money in the postal banks, as well as of procuring money orders, an arrangement that has proved of marked value to the class of men whose character for improvidence has ever been conspicuous. There also exists an arrangement under which the amount of scholarships awarded by the Technical Education Board of the London County Council are paid into the savings bank

NAVVIES AT A POST OFFICE SAVINGS BANK.

accounts of the scholars, as well as a plan for the deposit of the deferred pay of soldiers leaving the army. Both systems are much used.

The Life Insurance and Annuity business of the Post Office is now an important adjunct of the Savings

Bank Department. Originally instituted in 1864, under the auspices of Mr. Scudamore, the system was taken but little advantage of by the public, and for nearly twenty years it lingered with very meagre results accruing. In 1882 Mr. Fawcett determined upon popularising the system if possible, and acting upon an ingenious suggestion made by Mr. James J. Cardin, C.B., the present Comptroller and Accountant-General to the Post Office, he amalgamated it with the savings bank system. The scheme was legalised by the Government Annuities Act of 1882, and brought into operation in 1884. Briefly put, under that plan every insurer and annuitant becomes a Post Office Savings Bank depositor, and thus secures all the advantages which the system of that bank affords. He pays his premiums through his account as deposits, after the first premium has been paid, in such sums, and at such periods, as are most convenient to himself, always providing the full amount of the premium has been paid in by the time when it is due. This done, he has no further trouble. Various modifications and improvements have been made in the system from time to time with the object of extending its popularity, and the changes which have thus been effected have undoubtedly caused the Government Life Insurance and Annuity system to become more appreciated by those for whose advantage the system is designed. The published statistics show that during the last recorded year over 2000 annuities were purchased, and over 700 life insurance policies issued.

Amongst recent savings bank improvements may be mentioned the plan for withdrawals by telegraph. Under this plan, a depositor can withdraw sums of money from his deposit account by using the telegraph, providing, of course, he pays the charges for the telegrams involved. The want of a system of this kind had long been felt, and the convenience which the plan affords is much appreciated by the savings bank public. A similar plan, it should be stated, is in operation in connection with money orders, and has also given general satisfaction.

As may be supposed, in connection with a gigantic business like that of the Post Office Savings Bank, curious incidents often arise. Especially quaint and strange are some of the communications received. Here are a few instances for which we are indebted to Mr. Wilson Hyde, author of the interesting volume, "The Royal Mail." A depositor being asked to furnish particulars of his deposit account, the reply received from someone who had opened the letter on his behalf was to this effect: "He is a tall man, deeply marked with smallpox, has one eye, wears a billycock, and keeps a pen-booth at Lincoln Fair." The envelopes supplied to depositors, in which they send their books to headquarters, have within the flap a space provided for the depositor's address, and the request is printed beneath—"State here whether the above address is permanent." This request has called forth such rejoinders as these: "Here we have no continuing city;" "This is not our rest;" "Heaven is our home;" "Yes, *D.V.*" In one case the reply was, "No, *D.V.*, for the place is beastly damp and unhealthy;" while another depositor, being floored by the wording of the inquiry, wrote, "Doant know what permanent is!"

When deposit books are lost or destroyed, some explanation is usually forthcoming as to how the circumstance occurred, and some of these statements

are of a very curious kind.   Thus, a person employed
in a travelling circus accounted for the loss of his
book in these terms : " Last night when I was sleeping
in the tent, one of our elephants broke loose and tore
up my coat, in the pocket of which was my bank-
book, and ate part of it.   I enclose the fragments."
In another case the explanation was : " I think the
children has taken it out of doors and lost it, as they
are in the habit of playing shutalcock with the backs
of books."   Another depositor supposed his book " had
been taken from the house by our tame monkey ; "
while another vouchsafed the explanation that " I
was in the yard feeding my pigs.   I took off my coat
and left it down on a barrel ; while engaged doing so,
a goat in the yard pulled it down.   The book falling
out, the goat was chewing it when I caught her."   A
sergeant in the army lost his book " whilst in the act
of measuring a recruit for the army," which appears
to be an awkward insinuation as regards the recruit.
A needy depositor pledged his coat, forgetting to
withdraw his deposit-book, which was in one of the
pockets.   On applying for his coat, he found it had
been mislaid by the pawnbroker, and his book was
thus lost.   In another case the depositor accounted
for his loss " through putting the book in an old coat
pocket and selling the coat without taking out the
book again."   It was suggested that he should apply
to the purchaser of the coat, when he replied he had
been " to the rag merchant," but could find no trace
of the book.   One deposit-book is stated to have
been mutilated by a cat ; while another, which was
kept in a strong box in a pig-sty, had been destroyed
by the tenant—a pig.   In yet another case, the
depositor explained that " his little puppy of a dog

got hold of it and tore it all to pieces, not leaving so much as the number." A coastguardsman employed on the Sussex coast, writing shortly after the occurrence of some severe storms, explained that his book had been washed away with the whole of his household effects. In a case of mutilation of a book, the following account of the circumstance was given by the owner: "In the early part of last year I was taken seriously ill away from home; and having my bankbook with me, I wrote in the margin in red ink what was to be done with the balances in case of a fatal result, and as a precaution against its being wrongfully claimed on my recovery, I cut this out."

Such are some of the more curious instances of the loss of savings bank deposit-books—the loss being ordinarily ascribed, as Mr. Hyde explains, either to change of residence, to the book being dropped in the street, or its being burnt with waste-paper.

So far as the limits of a small volume will permit, the romance of the British Post Office has been traced, and as a veritable romance it reads; for within the comparatively short period of sixty years the department has grown from a concern of small dimensions and of but little account, the ways and system of which were uncertain and irregular, into a vast institution, the branches of which spread throughout the length and breadth of the country like the feelers of some great deep sea monster. But the history is nevertheless one of absolute facts, which, as is well-known, are generally stranger than fiction. The growth of our Post Office, in all its various ramifications, must ever be regarded as one of the most marvellous and stupendous records of the century that is closing in upon us. As a convenient and useful medium for the conveyance of letters and parcels, the transmission of telegrams, the remittance and banking of small sums of money, as well as the insurance of lives and the granting of annuities, the Post Office of Great Britain must ever be regarded as one of the first institutions of this country.

But the growth and development of the postal system mean more than this. They mean, indeed, the spread of education, the development of trade and commerce, and the knitting together in the bonds of unity and peace and of civilisation of all classes of Her Majesty's subjects. As a highly instructive lesson, and a fair and accurate illustration of the progress of civilisation and education, and of the condition of trade and commerce in this country during the Record Reign of the Queen, there could be no better record than that afforded by the history of the Post Office, a department which is more closely connected than any other perhaps with the daily life of the nation in its individuality.

The Postmaster-General's Report, which is probably the most popular annual publication of its kind, is a document always full of interesting reading, and is usually characterised by the narration of changes and improvements designed to afford increased facilities to the public. Government departments generally have the reputation of being machines hard to put in motion, and which, when in motion, work with extreme slowness. However true this may have been of the Post Office in by-gone years, that department cannot now be charged with the imputation. Those who aver, and there are such, that the Post Office is fast bound in red tape and enveloped in routine, speak without due reflection. In a huge business like that of the Post Office there must of course be certain methods and systems in performing the work, or else the business would soon fall into a chaotic state of confusion worse confounded. Absolute perfection is not to be attained in this world, and it would, therefore, be nothing short of miraculous if our great postal system were entirely free from imperfections and shortcomings. It is the endeavour of the authorities, however, to reduce these to a minimum, and anyone who knows the inner working of the department can well testify to the great exertions and untiring energy of the postal administration to this end.

This is an age of progress, and there can be no doubt that every endeavour is made by the Government to keep the Post Office well abreast of the times. Those in authority at St. Martin's le Grand are men of undoubted business capacity, and no one who knows them can question their desire, in administering their respective branches of the business, to study the wants and convenience of the public in regard to Post Office matters. If proof of this were wanting, we have but to look back over (say) the past twenty years, an epoch that must ever be regarded as one of the most important in Post Office history, owing to the manifold useful changes and reforms that have been wrought in the service. These have been the introduction and rapid extension of postal orders, and of the parcel post; the development of life insurance and savings bank business, the introduction of sixpenny telegrams, the acceleration of the mails in various directions, and a host of minor improvements of more or less importance, not forgeting the recent Jubilee reforms, all which have tended to bring the huge system into greater popularity with the public, and to make our Post Office the admiration of foreign nations.

The best measure of the success of the Post Office, however, is to be gained from its financial aspect. When in 1663 the Post Office revenue was settled by Act of Parliament upon the Duke of York and his heirs in perpetuity, the gross amount had increased to £21,000, and the net amount to £5000. In 1685 when, owing to the Duke having succeeded to the throne, it was necessary to re-settle the revenue upon the king, his heirs, and successors, the amount had risen to £65,000. It is interesting to note that the Post Office Accounts are preserved in an unbroken series from that year to the present time at St. Martin's le Grand. During the past two centuries the Post Office Revenue has increased at an enormous rate, and at the present time the gross revenue, including the telegraphs, is at the rate of nearly £15,000,000 a-year. The annual expenditure amounts to over £11,000,000, thus leaving a net revenue of close upon £4,000,000 with which to delight the heart of the Chancellor of the Exchequer.

THE END.

LORIMER AND GILLIES, PRINTERS, EDINBURGH.

Catalogue

OF

S. W. PARTRIDGE & CO.'S

POPULAR ILLUSTRATED BOOKS.

CLASSIFIED ACCORDING TO PRICES.

NEW BOOKS ARE MARKED WITH AN ASTERISK.

5s. each.

*The Dacoit's Treasure; or, In the Days of Po Thaw.
£200 Prize Story of Burmese Life. By Henry Charles Moore. Illustrated by Harold Piffard. Large Crown 8vo. Cloth extra, gilt top.

*A Gentleman of England. A Story of the Time of
Sir Philip Sydney. By Eliza F. Pollard, Author of "The White Dove of Amritzir," "Roger the Ranger," etc. Large Crown 8vo. Cloth extra, gilt top.

*Pilgrims of the Night. A Novel. By Sarah Doudney,
Author of "A Romance of Lincoln's Inn," "Louie's Married Life," etc. Frontispiece. Large Crown 8vo. Cloth extra, gilt top.

By G. MANVILLE FENN.

Illustrated by W. RAINEY, R.I., F. W. BURTON, etc.

*Cormorant Crag: A Tale of the Smuggling Days. By
G. Manville Fenn. Second Edition. Illustrated. Large Crown 8vo. Cloth extra, gilt top.

In Honour's Cause: A Tale of the Days of George the
First. By George Manville Fenn, Author of "Cormorant Crag," etc. Large Crown 8vo. Illustrated. Cloth extra, gilt top.

First in the Field: A Story of New South Wales. Large
Crown 8vo. Illustrated. Cloth extra, gilt top.

Steve Young; or, The Voyage of the "Hvalross" to the
Icy Seas. Large crown 8vo. Fully Illustrated. Cloth extra, gilt top.

Grand Chaco (The): A Boy's Adventures in an Unknown
Land. Large Crown 8vo. Fully Illustrated. Cloth extra, gilt top.

*Skeleton Reef (The). A Sea Story. By Hugh St· Leger, Author of "An Ocean Outlaw,' etc. Large Crown 8vo· Frontispiece. Cloth extra, gilt top.

*Lady Croome's Secret. By Marie Zimmermann, Author of "A Woman at Bay," etc. Illustrated. Large Crown 8vo. Cloth extra, gilt top.

*Scuttling of the "Kingfisher" (The). By Alfred E. Knight, Author of "Victoria: Her Life and Reign." Frontispiece. Large Crown 8vo. Cloth extra, gilt top.

*Missing Million (The): A Tale of Adventure in Search of a Million Pounds. By E. Harcourt Burrage, Author of "Whither Bound?" Frontispiece. Large Crown 8vo. Cloth extra, gilt top.

*Come, Break Your Fast: Daily Meditations for a Year. By Rev. Mark Guy Pearse. 544 pages. Large Crown 8vo. Cloth extra.

*Crystal Hunters (The): A Boy's Adventures in the Higher Alps. By G. Manville Fenn. New Edition. Illustrated. Large Crown 8vo. Cloth extra, gilt top.

Adventures of Don Lavington (The). By George Manville Fenn, Author of "Cormorant Crag," etc. New Edition. Illustrated by W. Rainey, R.I. Large Crown 8vo. Cloth extra, gilt top.

Hymn Writers and their Hymns. By Rev. S. W. Christophers. 390 pages. Crown 8vo. Cloth extra.

In Battle and Breeze. Sea Stories by Geo. A. Henty, G. M. Fenn, and W. Clark Russell. Illustrated. Large Crown 8vo. Cloth extra, gilt top.

More Precious than Gold. By Jennie Chappell. With Illustrations. Crown 8vo. Cloth extra, gilt edges.

Pilgrim's Progress (The). By John Bunyan. Illustrated with 55 full-page and other Engravings, drawn by Frederick Barnard, J. D. Linton, W. Small, and engraved by Dalziel Brothers. Crown 4to. Cloth extra, 3s. 6d. (Gilt edges, 5s.)

Romance of Lincoln's Inn (A). By Sarah Doudney, Author of "Louie's Married Life." Crown 8vo. Illustrated. Cloth.

Story of the Bible (The). Arranged in Simple Style for Young People. One Hundred Illustrations. Demy 8vo. Cloth extra, 3s. 6d. (Gilt edges, bevelled boards, 4s. 6d.)

Six Stories by "Pansy." Imperial 8vo. 390 pages. Fully Illustrated and well bound in cloth, with attractive coloured design on cover, and Six complete Stories in each Vol. Vols. 1, 2, 3, 4, and 5, 3s. 6d. each.

Two Henriettas (The). By Emma Marshall, Author of "Eaglehurst Towers," etc. Illustrated. Large Crown 8vo. Cloth extra, gilt top.

White Dove of Amritzir (The): A Romance of Anglo-Indian Life. By Eliza F. Pollard, Author of "Roger the Ranger," etc. Large Crown 8vo. Illustrated. Cloth extra, gilt top.

2s. 6d. each.

'ROMANCE OF COLONIZATION.''

Special attention is requested to this well-written and up to date Series of books on the development of British Colonization from its commencement to the present day.

Crown 8vo. Frontispiece. 320 pages. Cloth extra, 2s. 6d. each.

*I.—The United States of America to the Time of the Pilgrim Fathers. By G. Barnett Smith.

*II.—The United States of America to the Present Day. By G. Barnett Smith.

*III.—India. By Alfred E. Knight.

*Victoria: Her Life and Reign. By Alfred E. Knight. New Edition. Large Crown 8vo. 320 pages. Copiously Illustrated with most recent Portrait of Her Majesty, and numerous other Illustrations. Cloth extra, 2s. 6d.; fancy cloth, gilt edges, 3s. 6d.; half morocco, or half calf, marbled edges, net 7s. 6d.; full morocco, or calf, gilt edges, net 10s. 6d.

*John: A Tale of the Messiah. By K. Pearson Woods. Frontispiece. Crown 8vo. Cloth extra.

Brought to Jesus: A Bible Picture Book for Little Readers. Containing Twelve large New Testament Scenes, printed in colours, with appropriate letterpress by Mrs. G. E. Morton, Author of "Story of Jesus.' Size, 13½ by 10 inches. Handsome coloured boards with cloth back.

Bible Pictures and Stories. Old and New Testament. In one Volume. Bound in handsome cloth, with eighty-nine full-page Illustrations by Eminent Artists.

Light for Little Footsteps; or, Bible Stories Illustrated. By the Author of "Sunshine for Showery Days,' "A Ride to Picture Land," etc. With beautiful coloured Cover and Frontispiece. Full of Pictures.

Potters: Their Arts and Crafts. Historical, Biographical, and Descriptive. By John C. Sparkes (Principal of the Royal College of Art, South Kensington Museum), and Walter Gandy. Crown 8vo. Copiously Illustrated. Cloth extra, 2s. 6d.; art linen, gilt edges, 3s. 6d.

Story of Jesus. For Little Children. By Mrs. G. E. Morton, Author of "Wee Donald," etc. Many Illustrations. Imperial 16mo.

Sunshine for Showery Days: A Children's Picture-Book. By the Author of "A Ride to Picture Land," "Light for Little Footsteps," etc. Size 15½ by 11 inches. Coloured Frontispiece, and 114 full-page and other Engravings. Coloured paper boards, with cloth back.

Spiritual Grasp of the Epistles (The); or, an Epistle a-Sunday. By Rev. Charles A. Fox, Author of "Lyrics from the Hills," etc. Small Crown 8vo. Cloth boards. (Not illustrated.)

Upward and Onward. A Thought Book for the Threshold of Active Life. By S. W. Partridge. (Fourteenth Thousand.) Cloth boards, 2s. 6d. (Not Illustrated.)

2s. 6d. each (*continued*).

THE "RED MOUNTAIN" SERIES.

Crown 8vo. 320 Pages. Illustrated. Handsomely bound in cloth boards. 2s. 6d. each.

***The Wheel of Fate.** By Mrs. Bagot Harte, Author of "Wrongly Condemned," etc.

***A Polar Eden**: or, The Goal of the "Dauntless." By Charles R. Kenyon, Author of "The Young Ranchman," etc.

***Mark Seaworth**: A Tale of the Indian Archipelago. By W. H. G. Kingston, Author of "Manco, the Peruvian Chief."

***Vashti Savage**: The Story of a Gipsy Girl. By Sarah Tytler.

By Sea-Shore, Wood, and Moorland: Peeps at Nature. By Edward Step, Author of "Plant Life," etc.

Eaglehurst Towers. By Emma Marshall, Author of "Fine Gold," etc.

Eagle Cliff (The): A Tale of the Western Isles. By R. M. Ballantyne, Author of "Fighting the Flames," "The Lifeboat," etc.

Edwin, The Boy Outlaw; or, The Dawn of Freedom in England. A Story of the Days of Robin Hood. By J. Frederick Hodgetts, Author of "Older England," etc.

England's Navy: Stories of its Ships and its Services. With a Glance at some Navies of the Ancient World. By F. M. Holmes, Author of "Great Works by Great Men," etc.

Green Mountain Boys (The): A Story of the American War of Independence. By Eliza F. Pollard, Author of "True unto Death," "Roger the Ranger," etc., etc.

Great Works by Great Men: The Story of Famous Engineers and their Triumphs. By F. M. Holmes.

Lady of the Forest (The). By L. T. Meade, Author of "Scamp and I," "Sweet Nancy," etc.

Leaders Into Unknown Lands: Being Chapters of Recent Travel. By A. Montefiore, F.G.S., F.R.G.S. Maps, etc.

Lion City of Africa (The): A Story of Adventure. By Willis Boyd Allen, Author of "The Red Mountain of Alaska," etc.

Manco, The Peruvian Chief. By W. H. G. Kingston. New Edition. Illustrated by Launcelot Speed.

Olive Chauncey's Trust. By Mrs. E. R. Pitman, Author of "Lady Missionaries in Foreign Lands."

Roger the Ranger: A Story of Border Life among the Indians. By Eliza F. Pollard, Author of "Not Wanted," etc.

2s. 6d. each *(continued).*

THE "RED MOUNTAIN" SERIES *(continued).*

Red Mountain of Alaska (The). By Willis Boyd Allen, Author of "Pine Cones," "The Northern Cross," etc.

Slave Raiders of Zanzibar (The). By E. Harcourt Burrage, Author of "Gerard Mastyn," "Whither Bound?" etc.

Spanish Maiden (The): A Story of Brazil. By Emma E. Hornibrook, Author of "Worth the Winning," etc.

True unto Death: A Story of Russian Life and the Crimean War. By Eliza F. Pollard, Author of "Roger the Ranger."

Whither Bound? A Story of Two Lost Boys. By Owen Landor. With Twenty Illustrations by W. Rainey, R.I.

Young Moose Hunters (The): A Backwoods-Boy's Story. By C. A. Stephens. Profusely Illustrated.

2s. each.

*The Friends of Jesus. Illustrated Sketches for the young, of the Twelve Apostles, the Family at Bethany, and other of the earthly friends of the Saviour. Small 4to. Cloth extra.

Anecdotes in Natural History. By Rev. F. O. Morris, B.A. With numerous Illustrations. Fcap. 4to. Cloth extra.

Animals and their Young. By Harland Coultas. With Twenty-four full-page Illustrations by Harrison Weir. Fcap. 4to. Cloth gilt, bevelled boards.

Domestic Pets: Their Habits and Treatment. Anecdotal and Descriptive. Full of Illustrations. Fcap. 4to. Cloth extra.

Natural History Stories. By Mary Howitt. With Thirty-two full-page Engravings by Harrison Weir, L. Huard, etc., and numerous smaller Illustrations. Fcap. 4to. Cloth gilt, bevelled boards.

Our Dumb Companions. By Rev. T. Jackson, M.A. One Hundred and Twenty Illustrations. Fcap. 4to. Cloth extra.

Sunny Teachings. (New Series). A Bible Picture Roll containing Twelve beautifully Coloured Scripture Pictures selected from the New Testament. Mounted on roller.

Young Folk's Bible Picture Roll (The). Contains Twelve beautifully Coloured Pictures of Bible Subjects. Printed on good paper, and mounted on roller, with cord for hanging up.

Natural History Picture Roll. Consisting of Thirty-one Illustrated Leaves, with simple large-type Letterpress, suitable to hang up in the Nursery, Schoolroom, etc.

2s. each (*continued*).

THE HOME LIBRARY.

Crown 8vo. 320 pages. Handsome Cloth Cover. Illustrations.

*****Esther Dunbar**; or, Vengeance is Mine. By Eliza F. Pollard.

*****Tangled Threads.** By Esmá Stuart.

*****Ailsa's Reaping**; or, Grape-Vines and Thorns. By Jennie Chappell.

*****Petrel Darcy**; or, In Honour Bound. By T. Corrie.

*****Honor:** A Nineteenth Century Heroine. By E. M. Alford.

Avice: A Story of Imperial Rome. By Eliza F. Pollard.

Ben-Hur. By L. Wallace.

Better Part (The). By Annie S. Swan.

Brownie; or, The Lady Superior. By Eliza F. Pollard.

Bunch of Cherries (A). By J. W. Kirton.

Cousin Mary. By Mrs. Oliphant, Author of "Chronicles of Carlingford," etc.

Dr. Cross; or, Tried and True. By Ruth Sterling.

Dorothy's Training; or, Wild-Flower or Weed? By Jennie Chappell.

Edith Oswald; or, Living for Others. 224 pages. ⎱ By
Florence Stanley; or, Forgiving, because Much ⎰ Jane M.
Forgiven.   Kippen.

For Honour's Sake. By Jennie Chappell.

Gerard Mastyn; or, The Son of a Genius. By E. Harcourt Burrage.

Gerald Thurlow; or, The New Marshal. By T. M. Browne.

Household Angel (The). By Madeline Leslie.

Her Saddest Blessing. By Jennie Chappell.

Jacques Hamon; or, Sir Philip's Private Messenger. By Mary E. Ropes.

Living It Down. By Laura M. Lane.

Louie's Married Life. By Sarah Doudney.

Madeline; or, The Tale of a Haunted House. By Jennie Chappell.

Morning Dew-Drops. By Clara Lucas Balfour.

Mark Desborough's Vow. By Annie S. Swan.

Mick Tracy, the Irish Scripture Reader. By the Author of "Tim Doolan, the Irish Emigrant."

Naomi; or, The Last Days of Jerusalem. By Mrs. Webb.

2s. each.

THE HOME LIBRARY (*continued*).

Pilgrim's Progress (The). By John Bunyan. 416 pages. 47 Illustrations.

Strait Gate (The). By Annie S. Swan.

Uncle Tom's Cabin. By Harriet Beecher Stowe.

Woman at Bay (A). By Marie Zimmermann.

Without a Thought; or, Dora's Discipline. By Jennie Chappell.

Way in the Wilderness (A). By Maggie Swan.

By "PANSY."

Chrissy's Endeavour.
Three People.
Four Girls at Chautauqua.
An Endless Chain.
The Chautauqua Girls at Home.
Wise and Otherwise.

Ruth Erskine's Crosses.
Ester Ried.
Ester Ried Yet Yet Speaking.
Julia Ried.
The Man of the House.

Over 325,000 of these volumes have already been sold.

1s. 6d. each.

THE "WORLD'S WONDERS" SERIES.

A Series of Popular Books treating of the present-day wonders of Science and Art. Well written, printed on good paper, and fully illustrated. Crown 8vo, 160 pages. Handsome Cloth Cover.

*Romance of the Post Office: Its Inception and Wondrous Development. By Arch. G. Bowie.

*Marvels of Metals. By F. M. Holmes.

Miners and their Works Underground. By F. M. Holmes.

Triumphs of the Printing Press. By Walter Jerrold.

Astronomers and their Observations. By Lucy Taylor. With Preface by W. Thynne Lynn, B.A., F.R.A.S.

Celebrated Mechanics and their Achievements. By F. M. Holmes.

Chemists and their Wonders. By F. M. Holmes.

Engineers and their Triumphs. By F. M. Holmes.

Electricians and their Marvels. By Walter Jerrold.

Musicians and their Compositions. By J. R. Griffiths.

Naturalists and their Investigations. By George Day, F.R.M.S.

1s. 6d. each (*continued*).

NEW SERIES OF MISSIONARY BIOGRAPHIES.

Crown 8vo.　160 pages.　Cloth extra.　Fully Illustrated.

*Captain Allen Gardiner: Sailor and Saint.　By Jessie Page, Author of "Japan, its People and Missions," etc.

*Tiyo Soga: The Model Kaffir Missionary.　By H. T. Cousins, Ph.D., F.R.G.S.

Amid Greenland Snows; or, The Early History of Arctic Missions.

Among the Maoris; or, Daybreak in New Zealand.

Bishop Patteson, the Martyr of Melanesia.

By Jesse Page.

Congo for Christ (The): The Story of the Congo Mission. By Rev. J. B. Myers, Author of "William Carey," etc.

David Brainerd, the Apostle to the North American Indians.　By Jesse Page.

Henry Martyn: His Life and Labours—Cam- bridge, India, Persia.　By Jesse Page.

Japan: Its People and Missions.　By Jesse Page.

John Williams, the Martyr Missionary of Poly- nesia.　By Rev. James J. Ellis.

James Calvert; or, From Dark to Dawn in Fiji. By R. Vernon.

James Chalmers, Missionary and Explorer of Rarotonga and New Guinea.　By William Robson.

Lady Missionaries in Foreign Lands.　By Mrs. E. R. Pitman, Author of "Vestina's Martyrdom," etc.

Madagascar: Its Missionaries and Martyrs.　By William J. Townsend, Author of "Robert Morrison," etc.

Missionary Heroines in Eastern Lands.　By Mrs. E. R. Pitman, Author of "Lady Missionaries in Foreign Lands."

Reginald Heber, Bishop of Calcutta, Author of "From Greenland's Icy Mountains."　By A. Montefiore, F.R.G.S.

Robert Moffat, the Missionary Hero of Kuruman. By David J. Deane.

Samuel Crowther, the Slave Boy who became Bishop of the Niger.　By Jesse Page.

Thomas Birch Freeman, Missionary Pioneer to Ashanti, Dahomey, and Egba.　By Rev. John Milum, F.R.G.S.

William Carey, the Shoemaker who became the Father and Founder of Modern Missions.　By Rev. J. B. Myers.

NEW POPULAR BIOGRAPHIES.

Crown 8vo. 160 pages. Maps and Illustrations. Cloth extra.

*Fridtjof Nansen: His Life and Explorations. By J. Arthur Bain.

*Philip Melancthon: The Wittemberg Professor and Theologian of the Reformation. By David J. Deane, Author of "Two Noble Lives," etc.

General Gordon, the Christian Soldier and Hero. By G. Barnett Smith.

William Tyndale, the Translator of the English Bible. By G. Barnett Smith.

Heroes and Heroines of the Scottish Covenanters. By J. Meldrum Dryerre, LL.B., F.R.G.S.

Canal Boy who became President (The). By Frederic T. Gammon. Twelfth Edition. Thirty-fourth Thousand.

David Livingstone: His Labours and His Legacy. By Arthur Montefiore, F.G.S., F.R.G.S.

Four Heroes of India: Clive, Warren Hastings, Havelock, Lawrence. By F. M. Holmes.

Florence Nightingale, the Wounded Soldier's Friend. By Eliza F. Pollard.

Gladstone (W. E.): England's Great Commoner. By Walter Jerrold. With Portrait and thirty-eight other Illustrations.

John Knox and the Scottish Reformation. By G. Barnett Smith.

Michael Faraday, Man of Science. By Walter Jerrold.

"One and All." An Autobiography of Richard Tangye, of the Cornwall Works, Birmingham. With Twenty-one Original Illustrations by Frank Hewett. (192 pages.)

Sir John Franklin and the Romance of the North-West Passage. By G. Barnett Smith.

Slave and His Champions (The): Sketches of Granville Sharp, Thomas Clarkson, William Wilberforce, and Sir T. F. Buxton. By C. D. Michael.

Stanley (Henry M.), the African Explorer. By Arthur Montefiore, F.G.S., F.R.G.S.

Spurgeon (C. H.): His Life and Ministry. By Jesse Page.

Two Noble Lives: JOHN WICLIFFE, the Morning Star of the Reformation; and MARTIN LUTHER, the Reformer. By David J. Deane. (208 pages.)

Through Prison Bars: The Lives and Labours of John Howard and Elizabeth Fry, the Prisoner's Friends. By William H. Render.

Over 375,000 of these popular volumes have already been sold.

1s. 6d. each (*continued*).

THE BRITISH BOYS' LIBRARY.

A New Series of· 1s. 6d. books for boys.

Illustrated.   Crown 8vo.   Cloth extra.

*The Bell Buoy; or, The Story of a Mysterious Key
By F. M. Holmes.

*Jack. A Story of a Scapegrace. By E. M. Bryant.

*Hubert Ellerdale: A Tale of the Days of Wicliffe.
By.W. Oak Rhind.

THE BRITISH GIRLS' LIBRARY.

A New Series of 1s. 6d. books for girls.

Illustrated.   Crown 8vo.   Cloth extra.

*Sweet Kitty Claire. By Jennie Chappell.

*The Maid of the Storm: A Story of a Cornish
Village. By Nellie Cornwall.

*Mistress of the Situation (The). By Jennie
Chappell.

*Queen of the Isles. By Jessie M. E. Saxby.

NEW PICTURE BOOKS.

*Happy and Gay: Pictures and Stories for Every Day.
By D. J. D., Author of "Stories of Animal Sagacity," etc. With
8 coloured and 97 other Illustrations. Size 9 by 7 inches. Handsome coloured covers, paper boards with cloth backs.

*Pleasures and Joys for Girls and Boys. By
D. J. D., Author of "Anecdotes of Animals and Birds." With
8 coloured and 111 other Illustrations. Size 9 by 7 inches. Handsome coloured cover, paper boards and cloth back.

Anecdotes of Animals and Birds. By Uncle John.
With 57 full-page and other Illustrations by Harrison Weir, etc.
Fcap. 4to. 128 pages. Handsomely bound in paper boards, with Animal
design in 10 colours, varnished. (A charming book for the Young.)

Stories of Animal Sagacity. By D. J. D. A companion volume to "Anecdotes of Animals." Numerous full-page
Illustrations. Handsomely bound in paper boards, with Animal subject
printed in 10 colours, varnished.

1s. 6d. each (*continued*).

ILLUSTRATED REWARD BOOKS.

Crown 8vo.   160 pages.   Cloth extra.   Fully Illustrated.

Aileen; or, " The Love of Christ Constraineth Us." By Laura A. Barter, Author of " Harold ; or, Two Died for Me."

Claire; or, A Hundred Years Ago. By T. M. Browne, Author of " Jim's Discovery," etc.

Duff Darlington; or, An Unsuspected Genius. By Evelyn Everett-Green. With six Illustrations by Harold Copping.

Everybody's Friend; or, Hilda Danvers' Influence. By Evelyn Everett-Green, Author of " Barbara's Brother," etc.

Fine Gold; or, Ravenswood Courtenay. By Emma Marshall, Author of " Eaglehurst Towers," etc.

Her Two Sons. A Story for Young Men and Maidens. By Mrs. Charles Garnett, Author of " Mad John Burleigh," etc.

Jack's Heroism. A Story of Schoolboy Life. By Edith C. Kenyon.

Lads of Kingston (The). By James Capes Story.

Marigold. By L. T. Meade, Author of " Lady of the Forest," etc.

Minister's Money, The. By Eliza F. Pollard, Author of " True unto Death," etc.

Nobly Planned. By M. B. Manwell, Author of " Mother's Boy," etc.

Nature's Mighty Wonders. By Rev. Dr. Newton.

Nella; or, Not My Own. By Jessie Goldsmith Cooper.

Our Duty to Animals. By Mrs. C. Bray, Author of " Physiology for Schools," etc. Intended to teach the young kindness to animals. Cloth, 1s. 6d. ; School Edition, 1s. 3d.

Raymond and Bertha: A Story of True Nobility. By L. Phillips, Author of " Frank Burleigh ; or, Chosen to be a Soldier."

Rose Capel's Sacrifice; or, A Mother's Love. By Mrs. Haycraft, Author of " Like a Little Candle," " Chine Cabin," etc.

Satisfied. By Catherine M. Trowbridge.

Sisters-in-Love. By Jessie M. E. Saxby, Author of " Dora Coyne," " Sallie's Boy," etc. Illustrated by W. Rainey, R.I.

Ted's Trust; or, Aunt Elmerley's Umbrella. By Jennie Chappell, Author of " Who was the Culprit ?" " Losing and Finding."

Thomas Howard Gill: His Life and Work. By Eliza F. Pollard, Author of " Florence Nightingale," etc.

Tamsin Rosewarne and Her Burdens: A Tale of Cornish Life. By Nellie Cornwall.

ONE SHILLING REWARD BOOKS.

Fully Illustrated. 96 pages. Crown 8vo. Cloth extra.

*The Farm by the Wood. By F. Scarlett Potter, Author of "Phil's Frolic," etc.

*His Majesty's Beggars. By Mary E. Ropes, Author of "Bel's Baby," etc.

Always Happy; or, The Story of Helen Keller. By Jennie Chappell, Author of "Ted's Trust."

Arthur Egerton's Ordeal; or, God's Ways not Our Ways. By the Author of "Ellerslie House," etc.

Birdie and her Dog, and other Stories of Canine Sagacity. By Miss Phillips.

Birdie's Benefits; or, A Little Child Shall Lead Them. By Ethel Ruth Boddy.

Band of Hope Companion (The). A Hand-book for Band of Hope Members: Biographical, Historical, Scientific, and Anecdotal. By Alf. G. Glasspool.

Carol's Gift; or, "What Time I am Afraid I will Trust in Thee." By Jennie Chappell, Author of "Without a Thought," etc.

Brave Bertie. By Edith Kenyon, Author of "Jack's Heroism," "Hilda; or, Life's Discipline," etc.

Children of Cherryholme (The). By M. S. Haycraft, Author of "Like a Little Candle," "Chine Cabin," etc.

Cared For; or, The Orphan Wanderers. By Mrs. C. E. Bowen, Author of "Dick and his Donkey," etc.

Chine Cabin. By Mrs. Haycraft, Author of "Red Dave," "Little Mother," etc.

Dulcie Delight. By Jennie Chappell, Author of "Her Saddest Blessing," "For Honour's Sake," etc.

Frank Burleigh; or, Chosen to be a Soldier. By L. Phillips.

Frank Spencer's Rule of Life. By J. W. Kirton, Author of "Buy Your Own Cherries."

Grannie's Treasures, and How They Helped Her. By L. E. Tiddeman.

Hazelbrake Hollow. By F. Scarlett Potter, Author of "Phil's Frolic," etc. Illustrated by Harold Copping.

Harold; or, Two Died for Me. By Laura A. Barter.

How a Farthing Made a Fortune; or, "Honesty is the Best Policy." By Mrs. C. E. Bowen.

Jack the Conqueror; or, Difficulties Overcome. By the Author of "Dick and his Donkey."

Jemmy Lawson; or, Beware of Crooked Ways. By E. C. Kenyon, Author of "Jack's Heroism."

Jenny's Geranium; or, The Prize Flower of a London Court.

1s. each (*continued*).

SHILLING REWARD BOOKS (*continued*).

Jim's Discovery; or, On the Edge of a Desert. By
T. M. Browne, Author of "Dawson's Madge," etc.

Little Bunch's Charge; or, True to Trust. By Nellie
Cornwall, Author of "Tamsin Rosewarne," etc.

Losing and Finding; or, The Moonstone Ring. By
Jennie Chappell, Author of "Who was the Culprit?" etc.

Little Woodman and his Dog Cæsar (The). By
Mrs. Sherwood.

Little Bugler (The): A Tale of the American Civil War.
By George Munroe Royce. New Edition.

Lady Betty's Twins. By E. M. Waterworth, Author of
"Master Lionel," "Twice Saved," etc.

Marjory; or, What Would Jesus do? By Laura A. Barter,
Author of "Harold; or, Two Died for Me."

Marion and Augusta; or, Love and Selfishness. By
Emma Leslie, Author of "Ellerslie House," etc.

Mother's Chain (The); or, The Broken Link. By Emma
Marshall, Author of "Fine Gold; or, Ravenswood Courtenay," etc.

Nan ; or, The Power of Love. By Eliza F. Pollard, Author of
"Avice," "Hope Deferred," etc.

Old Goggles ; or, The Brackenhurst Bairns' Mistake. By
M. S. Haycraft, Author of "The Children of Cherryholme," etc.

Our Den. By E. M. Waterworth, Author of "Master
Lionel, that Tiresome Child."

Raymond's Rival; or, Which will Win? By Jennie
Chappell, Author of "Losing and Finding," etc.

Ronald Kennedy ; or, A Domestic Difficulty. By Evelyn
Everett-Green, Author of "Everybody's Friend," etc.

Recitations and Concerted Pieces for Bands of Hope,
Sunday Schools, etc. Compiled by James Weston.

Sweet Nancy. By L. T. Meade, Author of "Scamp and
I," "A Band of Three," etc.

Twice Saved ; or, Somebody's Pet and Nobody's Darling.
By E. M. Waterworth, Author of "Our Den," "Master Lionel," etc.

Temperance Stories for the Young. By T. S.
Arthur, Author of "Ten Nights in a Bar Room."

Three Runaways. By F. Scarlett Potter, Author of
"Phil's Frolic," "Hazelbrake Hollow," etc.

Una Bruce's Troubles. By Alice Price, Author of
"Hamilton of King's," etc. Illustrated by Harold Copping.

Under the Blossom. By Margaret Haycraft, Author
of "Like a Little Candle ; or, Bertrand's Influence," etc.

Wait till it Blooms. By Jennie Chappell, Author of
"Her Saddest Blessing," etc.

Who was the Culprit? By Jennie Chappell, Author
of "Her Saddest Blessing," "The Man of the Family," etc.

1s. each (*continued*).

POPULAR SHILLING SERIES.

Crown 8vo, well printed on good paper, and bound in attractive and tasteful coloured paper covers. Fully Illustrated.

Louie's Married Life. By Sarah Doudney.

The Strait Gate.

The Better Part.

Mark Desborough's Vow.

Grandmother's Child, and For Lucy's Sake.

} By Annie S. Swan.

Living it Down. By Laura M. Lane.

Eaglehurst Towers. By Mrs. Emma Marshall.

Without a Thought.

Her Saddest Blessing.

} By Jennie Chappell.

Fine Gold; or, Ravenswood Courtenay. By Emma Marshall.

The above can also be had in fancy cloth, price 1s. 6d.

CHEAP REPRINTS OF POPULAR STORIES FOR THE YOUNG.

Crown 8vo. 160 pages. Illustrated. Cloth boards, 1s. each.

*Rag and Tag: A Plea for the Waifs and Strays of Old England. by Mrs. E. J. Whittaker.

*Through Life's Shadows. By Eliza F. Pollard.

*Prue's Father; or, Miss Prothisa's Promise. By Ethel F. Heddle.

*The Little Princess of Tower Hill. By L. T. Meade.

*Clovie and Madge. By Mrs. G. S. Reaney.

*The Safe Compass and How it Points.

*The Best Things.

•Rays from the Sun.

} By Dr. Newton

Ellerslie House : A Book for Boys. By Emma Leslie.

Manchester House : A Tale of Two Apprentices. By J. Capes Story.

Like a Little Candle; or, Bertrand's Influence. By Mrs. Haycraft.

Violet Maitland ; or, By Thorny Ways. By Laura M. Lane.

Martin Redfern's Oath. By Ethel F. Heddle.

Dairyman's Daughter (The). By Legh Richmond.

1s. each (*continued*).

PICTURE BOOKS FOR THE YOUNG.

Fcap. 4to. With Coloured Covers, and Full of Illustrations.

*Frolic and Fun: Pictures and Stories for Every One. By Uncle Jack, Author of "Follow the Drum," etc. Four full-page coloured and numerous other Illustrations.

*Merry Playmates: Pictures and Stories for Little Folks. By C. D. M., Author of "Brightness and Beauty," etc. Four full-page coloured and numerous other Illustrations.

Follow the Drum: Pictures and Stories for Cheerful and Glum. By Uncle Jack, Author of "Bright Beams and Happy Scenes," etc. Four full-page coloured and numerous other illustrations.

Off and Away: Pictures and Stories for Grave and Gay. By C. D. M., Author of "Brightness and Beauty," etc. Four full-page coloured, and numerous other Illustrations.

Bible Pictures and Stories. Old Testament. By D. J. D., Author of "Pets Abroad," etc. With Forty-four full-page Illustrations. Coloured paper boards, 1s.; cloth gilt, 1s. 6d.

Bible Pictures and Stories. New Testament. By James Weston and D. J. D. With Forty-five beautiful full-page Illustrations by W. J. Webb, Sir John Gilbert, and others. New Edition. Fcap. 4to. Illustrated boards, 1s.; cloth, extra, 1s. 6d.

Bright Beams and Happy Scenes: A Picture Book for Little Folk. By J. D. Four full-page coloured and numerous other Illustrations. Coloured paper cover, 1s.; cloth, 1s. 6d.

Holiday Hours in Animal Land. (New Series.) By Uncle Harry. Four full-page coloured and numerous other Illustrations. Coloured paper cover, 1s.; cloth, 1s. 6d.

Merry Moments. A Picture Book for Lads and Lasses. By C. D. M. Four full-page coloured and many other Illustrations. Coloured paper cover, 1s.; cloth, 1s. 6d.

BOOKS BY REV. DR. NEWTON.

New and Cheap Edition. 160 pages. Crown 8vo. Prettily bound in cloth boards, 1s. each.

Bible Jewels. | Bible Wonders.
Rills from the Fountain of Life.
The Giants, and How to Fight Them.

Specially suitable for Sunday School Libraries and Rewards.

---

*Cicely's Little Minute. By Harvey Gobel. Long 8vo. Illustrated Title Page. Cloth extra. 1s. nett.

1s. each *(continued)*.

*The Master's Gifts to Women. By Mrs. Charlotte Skinner. Small 8vo. 112 pages. Cloth.

*The Master's Messages to Women. By Mrs. Charlotte Skinner. (Uniform with the above.)

*Some Secrets of Christian Living. Selections from the "Seven Rules" Series of Booklets. Small 8vo, cloth boards.

Brave and True. Talks to Young Men. By Thain Davidson, D.D. Small Crown 8vo. Cloth.

Daybreak in the Soul. By the Rev. E. W. Moore, M.A., Author of "The Overcoming Life." Imperial 32mo. 144 pages. Cloth.

My Guest Chamber; or, For the Master's Use. By Sophia M. Nugent. Imperial 32mo. 144 pages. Cloth.

Steps to the Blessed Life. Selections from the "Seven Rules" Series of Booklets. By Rev. F. B. Meyer, B.A. Small Crown 8vo, cloth boards.

Thoroughness: Talks to Young Men. By Thain Davidson, D.D. Small Crown 8vo. Cloth extra.

Women of the Bible. (Old Testament). By Etty Woosnam. Third Edition. Royal 16mo. Cloth.

Women of the Bible. (New Testament.) By the same Author. Royal 16mo. Cloth.

9d. each.

NINEPENNY SERIES OF ILLUSTRATED BOOKS.

96 pages. Small Crown 8vo. Illustrated. Handsome Cloth Covers.

*The Babes in the Basket; or, Daph and Her Charge.

*How Paul's Penny Became a Pound. By Mrs. Bowen, Author of "Dick and his Donkey."

*How Peter's Pound Became a Penny. By the same Author.

Paul, A Little Mediator. By Maude M. Butler.

A Flight with the Swallows. By Emma Marshall.

Boy's Friendship (A). By Jesse Page.

Bel's Baby. By Mary E. Ropes.

Benjamin Holt's Boys, and What They Did for Him. By the Author of "A Candle Lighted by the Lord."

Ben's Boyhood. By the Author of "Jack the Conqueror."

Ben Owen: A Lancashire Story. By Jennie Perrett.

Cousin Bessie: A Story of Youthful Earnestness. By Clara Lucas Balfour.

Dawson's Madge; or, The Poacher's Daughter. By T. M. Browne, Author of "The Musgrove Ranch," etc.

Five Cousins (The). By Emma Leslie.

9d. each *(continued)*.

Foolish Chrissy; or, Discontent and its Consequences. By Meta, Author of "Noel's Lesson," etc.

For Lucy's Sake. By Annie S. Swan.

Giddie Garland; or, The Three Mirrors. By Jennie Chappell.

Grandmother's Child. By Annie S. Swan.

Jean Jacques: A Story of the Franco-Prussian War. By Isabel Lawford.

John Oriel's Start in Life. By Mary Howitt.

Little Mother. By Margaret Haycraft.

Left with a Trust. By Nellie Hellis.

Letty; or, The Father of the Fatherless. By H. Clement, Author of "Elsie's Fairy Bells."

Love's Golden Key; or, The Witch of Berryton. By Mary E. Lester.

Master Lionel, that Tiresome Child. By E. M. Waterworth.

Man of the Family (The). By Jennie Chappell.

Mattie's Home; or, The Little Match-girl and her Friends.

Sailor's Lass (A). By Emma Leslie.

6d. each.

NEW SERIES OF SIXPENNY PICTURE-BOOKS.

Crown quarto. Fully Illustrated. Handsomely bound in paper boards, with design printed in Eight colours.

*****Sweet Stories Retold.** A Bible Picture-Book for Young Folks.

*****After School.**

*****Doggies' Doings and Pussie's Wooings.**

Under the Umbrella, Pictures and Stories for Rainy Days.

Rosie Dimple's Pictures and Stories for Tiny Folk.

Playful Pussies' Book of Pictures and Stories.

Little Snowdrop's Bible Picture-Book.

This New Series of Picture Books surpasses, in excellence of illustration and careful printing, all others at the price.

6d. each (*continued*).

THE "RED DAVE" SERIES.

New and Enlarged Edition, with Coloured Frontispieces. Handsomely bound in cloth boards.

Mother's Boy. By M.B. Manwell.

A Great Mistake. By Jennie Chappell.

From Hand to Hand. By C. J. Hamilton.

That Boy Bob. By Jesse Page.

Buy Your Own Cherries. By J. W. Kirton.

Owen's Fortune. By Mrs. F. West.

Only Milly; or, A Child's Kingdom.

Shad's Christmas Gift.

Greycliffe Abbey.

Red Dave; or, What Wilt Thou have Me to do?

Harry's Monkey: How it Helped the Missionaries.

Snowdrops; or, Life from the Dead.

Dick and his Donkey; or, How to Pay the Rent.

Herbert's First Year at Bramford.

Lost in the Snow; or, The Kentish Fisherman.

The Pearly Gates.

Jessie Dyson.

Maude's Visit to Sandybeach.

Friendless Bob, and other Stories.

Come Home, Mother.

Sybil and her Live Snowball.

Only a Bunch of Cherries.

Daybreak.

Bright Ben: The Story of a Mother's Boy.

THE MARIGOLD SERIES.

An entirely new and unequalled series of standard stories, printed on good laid paper. Imperial 8vo. 128 pages. Illustrated covers with vignette design printed in EIGHT COLOURS. *Price 6D. each,* NETT.

Pride and Prejudice. By JANE AUSTEN.

From Jest to Earnest. By E. P. Roe.

The Wide, Wide World. By SUSAN WARNER.

4d. each.

THE TINY LIBRARY.

Books printed in large type. Cloth.

Little Chrissie, and other Stories.

Harry Carlton's Holiday.

A Little Loss and a Big Find.

What a Little Cripple Did.

Bobby.

Matty and Tom.

The Broken Window.

John Madge's Cure for Selfishness.

The Pedlar's Loan.

Letty Young's Trials.

Brave Boys.

Little Jem, the Rag Merchant.

4d. each *(continued)*.

NEW FOURPENNY SERIES

of Cloth-bound Books for the Young. With Coloured Frontispieces. 64 pages. Well Illustrated. Handsome Cloth Covers.

Poppy; or, School Days at Saint Bride's.
Carrie and the Cobbler.
Dandy Jim.
A Troublesome Trio.
Perry's Pilgrimage.
Nita; or, Among the Brigands.
The Crab's Umbrella.
Sunnyside Cottage.
Those Barrington Boys.
Two Lilies.
The Little Woodman and His Dog Cæsar.
Robert's Trust.

CHEAP "PANSY" SERIES.

Imperial 8vo. 64 pages. Many Illustrations. Cover printed in Five Colours.

*Miss Priscilla Hunter and other Stories.
*Wild Bryonie.
*Avice. A Story of Imperial Rome.
A Young Girl's Wooing.
Spun From Fact.
A Sevenfold Trouble.
From Different Standpoints.
Those Boys.
Christie's Christmas.
Wise to Win; or, The Master Hand.
Four Girls at Chautauqua.
The Chautauqua Girls at Home.
Ruth Erskine's Crosses.
Ester Ried.
Julia Ried.
Ester Ried yet Speaking.
An Endless Chain.
Echoing and Re-echoing.
Cunning Workmen.
Tip Lewis and His Lamp.
The King's Daughter.
Wise and Otherwise.
Household Puzzles.
The Randolphs.
Mrs Solomon Smith Looking On.
Links in Rebecca's Life.
Three People.
Interrupted.
The Pocket Measure.
Little Fishers and their Nets
A New Graft on the Family Tree.
The Man of the House.

3d. each.

THE PRETTY "GIFT-BOOK" SERIES.

With Coloured Frontispiece, and Illustrations on every page. Paper boards, Covers printed in Five Colours and Varnished, 3d.; cloth boards, 4d. each.

My Pretty Picture Book.
Birdie's Picture Book.
Baby's Delight.
Mamma's Pretty Stories.
Tiny Tot's Treasures.
Papa's Present.
Pretty Bible Stories.
Baby's Bible Picture Book.
Ethel's Keepsake.
Out of School.
Pictures for Laughing Eyes.
Cheerful and Happy.

ILLUSTRATED MONTHLY PERIODICALS.

ONE PENNY MONTHLY.

THE BRITISH WORKMAN.

An Illustrated Paper containing brightly-written Articles and Stories on Religion, Temperance, and Thrift, short Biographical Sketches of Self-made Men, etc.
The Yearly Volume, with Coloured paper boards, cloth back, and full of Engravings, 1s. 6d. each ; cloth, 2s. 6d.

ONE HALFPENNY MONTHLY.

THE BAND OF HOPE REVIEW.

The Leading Temperance Periodical for the Young, containing Serial and Short Stories, Concerted Recitations, Prize Competitions, etc.
The Yearly Volume, with Coloured Cover and full of Engravings, cloth back, 1s. ; cloth gilt, 2s. each.

ONE PENNY MONTHLY.

THE CHILDREN'S FRIEND.

The Oldest and Best Magazine for Children. Excellent Serial and Short Stories, Prize Competitions, Puzzles, Music, etc. A charming Presentation Plate, in colours, is given away with the January number.
The Yearly Volume, Coloured paper boards, cloth back, 1s. 6d. ; cloth, 2s. ; gilt edges, 2s. 6d.

ONE PENNY MONTHLY.

THE INFANTS' MAGAZINE.

Full of charming Pictures and pleasant Rhymes to delight the little ones. Printed in large type. A splendid Coloured Presentation Plate given away with the January number.
The Yearly Volume, in Coloured paper boards, cloth back, 1s. 6d. ; cloth, 2s. ; gilt edges, 2s. 6d.

ONE PENNY MONTHLY.

THE FAMILY FRIEND and MOTHERS' COMPANION.

A beautifully Illustrated Magazine for the Home Circle, containing Serial and Short Stories by the leading writers of the day. Also crisply written Articles on popular subjects, Notes on Dressmaking, etc.
The Yearly Volume, with numerous Engravings, Coloured paper boards, cloth back, 1s. 6d. ; cloth, 2s. ; gilt edges, 2s. 6d.

ONE PENNY MONTHLY.

THE FRIENDLY VISITOR.

AN ILLUSTRATED GOSPEL MAGAZINE FOR THE PEOPLE.
Contains striking Gospel Stories and Articles, in large type, beautifully illustrated. An invaluable help to District Visitors, Mission Workers, etc.
The Yearly Volume, Coloured Cover, cloth back, 1s. 6d. ; cloth, 2s. ; gilt edges, 2s. 6d.

8 & 9, *PATERNOSTER ROW, E.C*